NOT OF THIS WORLD

Also by Simon R. Green

The Ishmael Jones mysteries

THE DARK SIDE OF THE ROAD *
DEAD MAN WALKING *
VERY IMPORTANT CORPSES *
DEATH SHALL COME *
INTO THE THINNEST OF AIR *
MURDER IN THE DARK *
TILL SUDDEN DEATH DO US PART *
NIGHT TRAIN TO MURDER *
THE HOUSE ON WIDOWS HILL *
BURIED MEMORIES *

The Gideon Sable series

THE BEST THING YOU CAN STEAL *
A MATTER OF LIFE AND DEATH *
WHAT SONG THE SIRENS SANG *

The Secret History series

PROPERTY OF A LADY FAIRE
FROM A DROOD TO A KILL
DR DOA
MOONBREAKER
NIGHT FALL

The Nightside series

JUST ANOTHER JUDGEMENT DAY
THE GOOD, THE BAD, AND THE UNCANNY
A HARD DAY'S KNIGHT
THE BRIDE WORE BLACK LEATHER

* *available from Severn House*

NOT OF THIS WORLD

Simon R. Green

**SEVERN
HOUSE**

First world edition published in Great Britain and the USA in 2023
by Severn House, an imprint of Canongate Books Ltd,
14 High Street, Edinburgh EH1 1TE.

Trade paperback edition first published in Great Britain and the USA in 2024
by Severn House, an imprint of Canongate Books Ltd.

severnhouse.com

British Library Cataloguing-in-Publication Data
A CIP catalogue record for this title is available from the British Library.

ISBN-13: 978-1-4483-0578-0 (cased)
ISBN-13: 978-1-4483-0579-7 (trade paper)
ISBN-13: 978-1-4483-0580-3 (e-book)

Typeset by Palimpsest Book Production Ltd.,
Falkirk, Stirlingshire, Scotland.

There is a world beneath the world, full of wonders and marvels just waiting to be stolen.

My name is Gideon Sable. These days.

There used to be someone else with that name: a master thief who specialized in stealing the kind of things that can't normally be stolen. Like a ghost's clothes, or the crown jewels from a country that never existed. But he disappeared, so I stole his identity. Now I am the legendary Gideon Sable: rogue operator, criminal mastermind and your last chance for a little quiet justice. Because the people I steal from always deserve it.

I have my own crew of specially talented individuals, to help me do the impossible. Annie Anybody, with a head full of other personas and a wardrobe of clothes and wigs and makeup that allow her to be anyone she wants. Lex Talon, who murdered two angels, from Above and Below, so he could steal their halos. Damned for all time, he chose to become the scariest agent of the Good that the Good ever had – just to spite Hell. Switch It Sally, that sweet and charming confidence trickster who can surreptitiously replace any small object with any other small object, so no one even knows they've been robbed until it's far too late. And Polly Perkins, exotic dancer, werewolf and the best tracker in the world.

Together, we steal incredible things from appalling people, to punish them for their crimes. And make ourselves incredibly rich in the process.

There is a world beneath the world: the underworld of crime.

ONE

Once We Had Stars in Our Eyes

Deep in the heart of London's Soho, there are people who walk the streets at night, and everyone gives them plenty of room, because they move like predators in a world of prey. Others stroll where they will without being bothered because no one knows they're there. No one sees or hears me unless I want them to, because I am a legendary master thief these days. And if I'm doing my job right, I can come and go and take whatever I fancy, and no one knows I was ever there.

Deep in the rotten heart of old Soho, tucked away in a sprawling warren of narrow lanes that can be darker than the deepest parts of the ocean, there are times when civilization just throws its hands in the air and gives up. In the early hours of the morning, when you're a long way from the dawn and it feels as if the night will never end, that's when the most unholy establishments and sleaziest nightclubs are just getting started. Pounding music blasts out of open doors, hot neon blazes in blatant come-ons, and the bouncers are outside throwing the punters in. This is Soho with the gloves off, offering all the pleasures and services no one in the daylight world would ever admit to wanting.

At three o'clock in the morning, the hour when most babies enter the world and the elderly just slip away, Soho lets its hair down and parties, and the night people come out to play. It's all there, waiting for you: sex and violence and rock and roll; magic and marvels and the occasional miracle; gods and monsters and everything in between . . . As long as it's clearly understood that not everything is necessarily what it seems.

You can find anything in Soho. If it doesn't find you first.

I went walking through the night while a cold wind gusted up and down the street, pushing people around like a bully in winter's clothing. I was on my way to discuss a new heist with a new client, but without my usual partner in crime, Annie Anybody. Because she kept saying it was time we retired. We were well enough off that we didn't need to work if we didn't want to, but of late I'd been feeling just a bit bored and more than a little restless. I didn't steal a legendary thief's name and reputation just so I could put my feet up and take it easy. I missed the excitement and the challenge of stealing from the rich and keeping it, and above all kicking the bad guys where it hurt them the most: right in their bulging wallets. I lived to take down the villains who thought they were untouchable and make them pay for the suffering they caused. For justice, revenge and the sheer thrill of it.

I paused before a shop window, so I could check out my current look. Tall, dark-haired and handsome enough to run most cons, I was wearing a black leather blazer, a white shirt and grey slacks. Because colours get you noticed. I put my faith in clothes that hold more pockets than anyone would expect, packed full of surprises and dirty tricks, but still loose enough that they won't get in the way if I suddenly find it necessary to sprint for the horizon. I nodded to my reflection. It winked back, because it was that sort of area, and I set off again with a spring in my step and honest larceny in my heart.

The Church of St Giles the Apostate loomed up before me, a dark and brooding last port in a storm that didn't give a damn about offering hope or solace to those in need. Already old when Jesus of Nazareth visited Londinium on his gap year, the church had hidden its true nature behind many names, but people who needed its particular helping hand could always find someone to tell them where it was.

People came to St Giles the Apostate so they could gain access to the ancient stone crypt concealed beneath it. The Whispering Gallery, where no one would overhear what you had to say – not even God. Where all the deals and bargains are made that are none of Heaven or Hell's business. I'd been there once before, to discuss my first job as Gideon Sable. A complicated affair, involving a man with no soul; a man with many, not all his own; and a witch who loved them both, after a fashion. Some jobs you just know aren't going to work out well for anyone.

I stopped a cautious distance away, concealing myself in the shadows between two black-iron street lamps, and looked the church over carefully. My anonymous invitation had arrived on a handwritten card that just appeared out of nowhere inside my very own magical shop. (Purveyor of wonders and marvels, at almost reasonable prices.) Such a thing shouldn't have been possible, given that my security measures include mantraps for the soul, curse-shaped landmines and a stuffed grizzly bear that acts as doorman and bouncer. Customers are always welcome, but anyone who approaches my shop with bad intent will be lucky to live long enough to regret it.

The card invited me to attend the Whispering Gallery, on this date and at this ungodly hour, where I was assured I would learn something to my advantage. As the great man said, I can resist everything except temptation, so here I was outside St Giles'. Intrigued, but cautious. No lights showed at any of the stained-glass windows, and no one went anywhere near the only door. The church felt empty, and empty for a reason.

Twilight tourists bustled up and down the street, intent on their own personal damnations. They paid no attention to the church, apart from making sure they didn't stray too close, as though avoiding a big dog that would bite if it got the chance. I let them pass, as my attention became fixed on a slim motionless figure studying the scene from some extremely dark shadows further down the street. Their interest had to be as professional as mine because regular people aren't supposed to stand that still for so long. I smiled slowly as I decided I needed to know who this was and what was going on, before I committed myself to anything.

When I took over the identity of Gideon Sable, the first thing I did was break into the original's private safe deposit box. (I didn't think he'd mind, given that he was so thoroughly missing.) Inside the box, I found a number of useful items that went a long way to explaining how the original Gideon became a legend. One was a ballpoint pen that could pause

Time and allow me to move freely through the motionless world that exists between the tick and tock of the world's clock.

I removed the pen from my jacket pocket, glanced casually up and down the street, and then hit the button. The dull amber streetlight immediately descended into a sullen crimson glow of infra-red. There was no movement and no sound anywhere, just a sensation of endlessly falling dust. I left my shadows and headed straight for the other observer, forcing my way past the stubborn resistance of the frozen world. I had to do this as quickly as possible because there wasn't any air to breathe. And because there were dangers to using the pen. I found a note in the safe deposit box: *Don't use it too often. They'll notice.* I had no idea who *They* were, and I really didn't want to find out the hard way.

I eased to a halt in front of the figure lurking in the shadows, and when I made out their features, the surprise was almost enough to drive the last air out of my lungs. It was my love and partner, Annie Anybody, in her persona as the girl adventurer Melody Mead. She was wearing a coal-grey catsuit zipped right up to the chin, along with a belt of useful things in pouches, topped off with a severe black wig that gave her face a sardonic, distrustful look. Her gaze was fixed on the church, like a hawk upon its prey.

Annie wasn't supposed to be here. She'd told me recently that she'd retired from the bad old days of graft and con, or so she said, which was why I hadn't told her about the card or the invitation. And she certainly wasn't supposed to be Melody Mead – a legendary troublemaker always ready to throw herself into some new danger.

Even though my lungs were straining for air, I took a moment to consider the situation. Why had Annie come to St Giles' in a persona more useful for storming barricades than meeting a client? And why hadn't she told me she was coming? Unfortunately, there was only one way to find out. I braced myself and hit the button on the pen. Time restarted, the amber street light returned, and Melody almost jumped out of her catsuit when I suddenly appeared right in front of her. I showed her my most engaging smile.

'Hello, Mel. What's a nice girl like you doing in a neighbourhood like this?'

She glared right back at me. 'Gideon! Why do you always have to turn up and spoil my fun?'

'I was invited here to meet someone I don't know, to discuss doing something that hasn't been explained to me yet,' I said. 'A card turned up at the shop, directing me to the Whispering Gallery.'

'Snap,' said Melody, and a card appeared in her hand.

I produced mine, and we compared them. The message was identical, in the same elegant handwriting. Melody's frown deepened into a scowl, and she made her card disappear with a flick of the hand.

'I was here first. It's my heist.'

'You wish,' I said, making my card vanish without moving my fingers. 'Why you, Melody?'

She tossed her head dismissively. 'I'm the adventurous one. Go home, Gideon. I can do this without you.'

I smiled easily because I knew that would irritate her the most. 'You wouldn't last five minutes inside St Giles' without me – and you know it.'

She lashed out with a blow that would have rattled my brain if I hadn't seen it coming. But I knew Melody of old, which was why I hadn't put the time pen away. The moment her stance changed, I hit the button and Time crashed to a halt, freezing Melody in mid-motion. I stepped carefully to one side and set Time moving again. Melody stumbled forward, caught off balance, and would have fallen if I hadn't caught her arm to hold her up. She jerked free and raised her fist again, only to stop when I showed her the pen in my hand.

'You can't get rid of me that easily, Mel, so just get used to the idea that you have a partner in this deal. You never know, I might come in handy.'

'Maybe,' said Melody. 'As a human shield. All right, let's do this. What's your plan? You always have a plan.'

'Plans require preparation,' I said. 'And since I had no idea what to prepare for, I thought I'd just wing it.'

I took one last look up and down the narrow lane, to make sure no one else was taking an undue interest in St Giles'.

The few late-night wanderers seemed to have more important matters on their minds, so I strolled casually over to the church and arrived in front of the door as if by accident. I tried the handle, just on the off chance, but it didn't want to know. Melody sniffed loudly behind me.

'It's locked. I already checked.'

'Nothing's locked when I'm around,' I said cheerfully. I produced my special skeleton key, another helpful little item from the safe deposit box, and the ancient lock gave in with only the slightest persuasion. I eased the door open and then thrust out an arm to prevent Melody from pushing past me. I made her wait a moment, while I checked that everything was quiet, and then led the way in. The empty church fell away before me, grim and forbidding. I took another moment to carefully close and lock the door behind us, and Melody hit me with another loud sniff.

'Paranoid, much?'

'We don't want to be interrupted, do we?'

Rows of stark wooden pews, without style or ornamentation or any trace of padding, eventually gave way to a bare stone altar at the far end of the church. There were no crucifixes, no statues, no Christian imagery at all. Even the stained-glass windows were nothing more than colourful patterns. St Giles' reminded me of one of those jungle insects that can look exactly like bits of vegetation until they jump on their prey. Half a dozen candles provided helpful pools of light, pushing back the smothering gloom, but there was still an uneasy tension in the air, a feeling that something was watching and listening. But it felt cold and remote enough that I decided it was unlikely to interfere.

'Please tell me you know the way to the Whispering Gallery,' said Melody.

'Of course,' I said. 'I know everything. Or, at least, everything that matters.'

'Is it true that anything said in the Gallery remains private, even from God?'

I shrugged. 'The general feeling seems to be that sometimes Heaven and Hell prefer not to know things, so they won't have to get involved.'

'It's probably just another con,' said Melody. 'This is Soho, after all.'

'No,' I said. 'Not in here, it isn't.'

She looked at me sharply, picking up on the cold certainty in my tone, and stopped talking.

I led the way down the aisle, to an unobtrusive side door tucked away behind the altar. I had my skeleton key ready, but the door wasn't locked. It opened on to a rough stone staircase that went spiralling down into the depths, with more candles to illuminate the way. I started down the dusty steps, and this time Melody was happy to let me go first, so if anything bad should happen, it would happen to me before it got to her. We descended the stone steps in silence, until finally Melody leaned forward so she could murmur in my ear.

'Who's responsible for keeping all these candles lit?'

'Beats me,' I said. 'The church doesn't have any staff that I know of.'

'I thought you knew everything?'

'This is the Church of St Giles the Apostate,' I said. 'Where secrets come as standard.'

The steps finally spiralled to a halt, and we emerged into a long stone crypt. Not the Gallery – not yet – just an old-time resting place for the honoured dead. Two rows of medieval tombs, with stylized human figures reclining on the lids. Knights and crusaders in full armour, cast in cold white marble, clutching long swords to their chests as though they expected to take their war with them into the afterlife. The faces were so perfectly realized as to seem almost inhuman, and the open eyes stared into infinity.

It was deathly silent, and the air was flat and still, as though nothing had disturbed it in a long time. Hardly surprising. No one here had any interest in being visited by family or mourners.

'OK . . . This isn't even a little bit creepy,' said Melody, keeping her voice low so as not to attract attention. 'Who thought a bunch of knights in armour would come in handy down here?'

'Someone who thought the church could use a few

watchdogs,' I said, just as quietly. 'Don't get too close to any of them; they sleep but lightly while they wait.'

Melody looked at me. 'What?'

I pointed at the Latin sign on the wall. 'A warning – or a threat.'

I set off down the narrow aisle, careful to maintain a respectful distance from the motionless figures stretched out on their tombs, but Melody had to be Melody, of course. She stopped by one particularly impressive figure, stared thoughtfully at the jewels encrusted on his sword hilt and leaned over for a closer look. I moved quickly in and hauled her away, and she scowled at me ferociously as she jerked her arm free.

'Stop doing that! I was just taking an interest!'

'Really not a good idea,' I said. 'All of these knights have incredibly big swords. And we don't.'

'Oh, come on! They're only statues!'

And then she broke off, as the head of the knight she'd been looking at slowly turned and fixed her with its cold, cold eyes. Melody's hands went to the pouches at her belt and then fell away again as she realized she had nothing that could protect her. The marble figure sat up, swung his legs over the side of the tomb and stood up. Dust and cobwebs fell away from the huge shape, as though they no longer had a hold on him. Massive and bulky in his medieval armour, the knight's every movement was still eerily smooth. He started towards us, holding his long sword out before him. Implacable and relentless, like some ancient engine following orders laid down long ago. Melody and I backed away, and the figure cast in marble came after us.

'Should we run?' said Melody. 'Running feels like a really good idea.'

'We wouldn't get far,' I said. 'That thing might be a lot heavier than us, but it doesn't have human limitations.'

'Don't you have anything you can use against it?'

'Don't you?' I said. 'You're the one with all the pouches on your belt.'

'I wasn't expecting to have to fight half a ton of solid marble, holding a bloody big sword!'

'That's always been your problem, Mel,' I said. 'You never think ahead.'

The knight surged forward, raised his sword and brought it hammering down, and the heavy blade whistled as it cut through the air. Melody and I threw ourselves in opposite directions, and the sword slammed into the stone floor, sending fragments flying in all directions. Melody and I quickly regained our balance, but our desperate reactions had brought us too close to the other tombs, and now more of the marble figures were stirring.

'Don't you have any weapons?' said Melody.

'I don't do weapons,' I said. 'That's why I have plans.'

'Didn't you have one for being down here?'

'Yes,' I said. 'But it involved you not being here.'

The long sword came sweeping around in a vicious arc, and we had to drop right down to duck under it. One of the other marble knights stepped down from his tomb with slow deliberate movements, and his cold gaze promised terrible retribution for having to lie still for so long.

'Use the time pen!' said Melody.

'I already thought of that! Even if we could slip past them, they'd never stop coming after us!'

'Then think of something else!'

I grinned suddenly. The other knight coming to life had given me an idea. I darted forward and placed myself exactly between the two marble figures, and they both attacked me at the same time. I dropped down on one knee, and each sword slammed into the opposing knight. Supernaturally sharp edges sank deep into aged marble, and both figures staggered and almost fell under the sheer force of the impacts. I scrambled backwards on my hands and knees, and lacking any visible threat, the two knights continued their assault on each other.

They pounded away with their heavy swords, gouging and shattering the chalk-white marble until deep cracks radiated across both knights. They lurched back and forth in the cramped space, battling each other like stubborn drunks, until suddenly they collapsed, falling apart in a rain of jagged pieces until there was nothing left of them but piles of marble wreckage. Half a detached face rocked slowly back and forth, staring accusingly at me with its empty eyes, and a cold white hand clutched convulsively at nothing, but it wasn't long before all the pieces lay still and lifeless on the cold stone floor.

I helped Melody to her feet and then held her firmly, until one by one the remaining marble figures grew still again, returning to their long rest. I let go of Melody, and she nodded curtly to me.

'Good plan.' It was as close as she could get to an apology.

'It's what I do,' I said. 'Now let us please stick to the middle of the aisle and not do the tourist thing . . . and maybe we can get to the Whispering Gallery without upsetting any more of the Gallery's supernatural guardians.'

Melody looked at me sharply. 'There are more guard dogs?'

'Wouldn't surprise me at all. Let's just hope we haven't already triggered some silent alarm.'

'You always have to look on the bad side of things.'

'That's how I've lasted this long.'

Slowly, step by careful step, we made our way down the narrow aisle and out at the far end. The crypt gave way to a labyrinth of narrow stone passageways, and I stopped well short of the entrance. I felt like a mouse confronted by some mad scientist's maze, with no idea of what was being tested. Melody started to push impatiently past me, but I just hauled her back again. She yanked her arm free and glared at me.

'Stop doing that!'

'Stop giving me reasons to,' I said. 'We have a problem. This maze wasn't here the last time I came this way.'

Melody looked suspiciously at the stone passageways. 'You mean someone built all of this since then?'

'More likely we did trip some kind of alarm after all, and this appeared as a result.'

Melody considered the maze thoughtfully. 'Does this still lead to the Whispering Gallery?'

'Good question,' I said. I took out my special compass, the one that always points to what I need, and the needle immediately indicated one particular path.

'Follow me,' I said. 'And keep your eyes open for booby traps.'

'I think this is the booby trap,' said Melody.

'Either way,' I said, 'I set the pace. And don't give me a hard time, because if you do, I swear I will drag you back the way we came, throw you out of the church and lock the door in your face.'

Melody looked at me. 'You would, wouldn't you?'

'If that's what it took to save your life, believe it,' I said. 'We're on a job here. Try to act like a professional.'

She nodded curtly, and when I entered the maze, she stuck so close behind me that she was almost treading on my heels. I followed the compass needle through a series of narrow passageways, and it wasn't long before I'd lost all sense of direction. The walls appeared to be thick and heavy: rough pitted stone covered in deeply etched runes. I had to wonder where the church had found this maze before it brought it here. My compass needle jerked this way and that, as it searched out the best route to the exit, and I kept up a steady pace because I could feel a threat even if I couldn't see one. Most mazes have a minotaur, but some don't need a monster to be dangerous. There was a sudden low grinding noise, of stone scraping against stone, and then the walls on either side of us began to edge forward. Our narrow world was closing in on us, with bad intent.

'They're going to crush us!' said Melody.

'I had worked that out!' I said. 'Try to stop them!'

I pressed my hands against the nearest wall and pushed hard, putting my back into it, but I couldn't even slow the wall's advance. Melody produced a handful of wooden wedges from one of her pouches and tried to force one into the gap between the wall and the floor, but it just spat the wedge out and kept pressing forward like a slow-motion avalanche.

'I don't suppose you've got some plastic explosive?' I said.

Melody shook her head quickly and threw a quick glance back the way we'd come.

'Any chance we could make it to the opening?'

I didn't need to glance behind me. 'We'd never get there.'

'Is it much further to the exit?'

'No way of telling.'

'Then what are we going to do?'

'When in doubt,' I said, 'cheat.'

I took out the time pen, took a deep breath and nodded to Melody to do the same, and then took her by the hand. I hit the button, and the dim crimson hue suffused the scene. The advancing walls slammed to a halt, and the two of us sprinted down the narrow passageway, with me using all my strength to keep us moving through the terrible inertia of the frozen world. Melody clung tightly to my hand as we pounded along, because she was only free from Time's hold as long as she remained in close contact.

All too soon, I was having to fight for every step as we forced our way through the frozen moment. I was using up my air a lot more quickly than I'd hoped. The passage had stopped branching, which I hoped meant that when we reached the far end, we'd be out of the maze, but it was becoming increasingly clear that we weren't going to reach it in time. So I hit the pen and let Time crash back into motion. Melody and I both gasped for air as the walls ground forward again. I almost fell, and Melody had to grab my arm to hold me up.

'Don't you dare wimp out on me! We're almost there!'

'Go,' I said. My head was swimming, and my legs were shaking. I put a hand on the small of Melody's back and gave her a good shove. 'Run!'

For once, she didn't argue. She sprinted down the narrowing passageway, while I reached out and placed both hands flat against the advancing walls. I straightened my arms and then locked them in position, holding the walls back to buy Melody some time. First my arm muscles and then my shoulders filled with agony as the pressure increased, but I was damned if I'd give an inch until Melody was safe. Because when the walls finally did come together, it would be a slow, horrid, grinding death. Finally, one of my feet slipped and I was thrown off balance. I dropped to one knee, my aching arms hanging limply at my sides. I forced myself back on to my feet and stumbled forward as best I could.

The walls were so close now that they pressed against my shoulders, and I had to turn sideways just to keep going. My head hung down, sweat dripping off my face on to the floor. It took everything I had to just keep putting one foot in front of the other. Melody yelled my name, and I looked up to see her standing outside the slowly closing gap at the end of the passageway. *Good*, I thought tiredly. *At least one of us made it.*

'Gideon! Don't you dare give up!' Melody glared fiercely at me through the narrowing gap. 'Get your arse moving, or I swear I'll come back in there and get you!'

Well, I thought. *Can't have that. She'd never let me hear the end of it.*

I drove myself on as the walls moved in for the kill. I had to squeeze through sideways, the walls pressing against my chest and back. Only sheer force of will kept me going, and I was so exhausted that I was genuinely surprised when I found the exit right in front of me. Melody reached out and hauled me through a gap so narrow I wouldn't have thought a supermodel could make it, and we both collapsed in a heap on the far side of the maze. We held each other tightly, while the walls slammed together with spiteful cheated force.

For a while, we just lay there on the cold stone floor, holding on to each other. It felt like old times, when Annie and I would work together to defy everything the world could throw at us. But the moment I was breathing normally again, Melody pushed me away and scrambled up on to her feet. She didn't even glance at me as she brushed herself down and looked around.

'Come on,' she said. 'You can't just lie there all day. We have work to do.'

I forced myself up on to my feet, taking care not to let her see how much the effort cost me.

'We don't want to rush this,' I said. 'Things have changed too much down here for my liking.'

Melody shook her head stubbornly. 'The longer we spend here, the more chances our enemies have to throw things at us.'

I had to raise an eyebrow. 'Enemies? Who did you have in mind?'

'I don't know! Just move your useless arse, before I introduce it to my boot.'

I looked at her. 'Perhaps you should let Annie out for a while. We could use her common sense.'

Melody stared at me. 'Who's Annie?'

I didn't know what to say. Annie's personas were only ever aspects of herself, created with wigs and costumes and makeup. They were never supposed to be separate people. Melody glowered at me.

'How do we get to the Gallery?'

I consulted my compass again, and the needle pointed straight ahead. When I looked up, there was a perfectly ordinary door in the wall ahead of us that I would have sworn wasn't there a moment before. I pointed it out, and Melody strode right up to the door, kicked it open and marched through. I shook my head and went in after her.

The Whispering Gallery was just as I remembered. A stone cavern with roughly hewn walls, a bare floor and a surprisingly high ceiling. As though to give whatever words were spoken room to breathe. More of the ubiquitous candles shed a warm glow from a series of wall niches. The door had already closed itself behind us, and I had a sudden sense of being utterly cut off from the world – as though, by entering the Gallery, Melody and I had stepped outside of everything we knew.

An old man was standing quietly in the middle of the cavern, studying us with sharp, cold eyes. He stood straight-backed and stiff-necked, as though he'd been waiting for some time and was perfectly prepared to go on waiting for as long as it took. He was small and compact, wearing what had once been a very expensive suit. The years had made it shabby, and it hung loosely around his aged frame, but the old school tie was still tightly knotted. His face was heavily lined, dominated by a noble brow and a beak of a nose. He looked at me steadily, and his thin lips twitched in what was probably meant as a smile. I moved over to stand before him. Just to be contrary, Melody left me to it and went prowling around the Gallery, glaring suspiciously at everything.

The old man ignored her, his icy blue eyes fixed on me. 'So you're the legendary Gideon Sable; I thought you'd be more impressive.'

'I am,' I said. 'I just prefer to hide my genius under a bushel.'

The old man barely nodded. 'I am Professor Neal Sharpe. I summoned you here to discover if you were as good as your reputation suggested. Because the job I have in mind will test even your skills to their limits.'

'How did you find out about me?' I said. 'And my companion?'

'When you've lived as long as I have, you know people who know people,' Sharpe said calmly. 'So you can always find someone to tell you what you need to know.'

Melody fell in beside me for a moment, so she could hit Sharpe with her best forbidding stare.

'Why are we here?'

'I need you to break into one of the most heavily guarded places in the world and steal something that can't normally be stolen,' said Sharpe.

I had to smile. 'The usual.'

Melody sniffed loudly. 'Show off.'

She went back to prowling around the cavern. I shrugged at Sharpe, to make it clear her behaviour was nothing to do with me.

'Why present us with separate invitations?'

'In case one of you wasn't interested,' said Sharpe. 'I have to say, I was impressed by the way you worked together tonight.'

'You've been watching us all this time?' I said.

'Of course. Think of your journey here as an audition.'

I took a step forward. To his credit, he didn't flinch.

'Are you responsible for the dangers we encountered?'

'I might have given them a nudge in the right direction. So I could observe the two of you in action.'

'I could make a hole in the wall with you,' Melody said loudly.

'Please don't,' said Sharpe. 'Not until you've heard what the job entails.'

'How did you get into the Whispering Gallery?' I said.

'I know people who know people,' said Sharpe.

'That's not an answer,' I said.

He showed me his twitch of a smile again. 'You have your secrets, and I have mine.'

'Let's start with who you are,' I said.

'I used to be Head of the British Rocketry Group, back in the fifties. Oh, yes, there really was such a thing. After the war ended, it was a time of triumph and optimism; it seemed like the whole universe was just waiting for us to come and explore it. We were doing so well . . . until it all went horribly wrong.'

'Why have I never heard about any of this?' I said.

'We decided early on that our achievements were none of the world's business,' said Sharpe. 'All of our rockets were launched from remote and isolated locations, under conditions of extreme secrecy.'

'So Britain was exploring outer space in the fifties?' I said. 'That's amazing . . . But where did you get the money to fund all of this? I thought the country was broke, after the war?'

'We chanced upon a crashed alien starship,' said Sharpe. 'And reverse-engineering its technology gave us the break-throughs we needed. We put a man in orbit around the Earth way ahead of the Russians and made landings on the Moon and Mars while the Americans were still playing catch-up. We had just started drawing up plans for planetary bases, to make it clear to the rest of the world that space belonged to us . . . when everything fell apart.'

Melody appeared beside me again. 'What does any of this have to do with why we're here?'

'I need you to acquire something left over from that time,' said Sharpe. 'Something so well guarded that only extra-ordinarily talented thieves such as yourselves could get anywhere near it.'

'What is it you want us to steal?' I said.

'You've heard of Area 51?' said Sharpe. 'The secret base where the Americans store their crashed flying saucers. Britain had one, too. The Preserve was originally set up to archive all the triumphs and by-products from the British Rocketry Group considered too dangerous to be publicly acknowledged. But it ended up as a dumping ground for everything the govern-ment wanted to bury or forget. The Preserve is where they locked away the last traces of a mission that went so badly wrong it shut the Rocketry Group down forever. All our dreams, flushed down the toilet, just because the government lacked the nerve to press on . . .'

His voice faded away, and he stared at nothing for a long moment, his gaze lost in the past.

'What happened?' I said. 'Did you make contact with . . . something?'

Sharpe pulled himself together. 'Space is vast, but it's not empty. Things exist in the cold vacuum that we have no way of detecting; they are without form or mass, just waiting to encounter some physical form of life so they can join with it and make themselves manifest in our reality. Swimming like sharks, in an ocean of stars. Some are monsters, some are angels . . . but most are simply beyond our comprehension.

'This particular rocket was on its way to Venus when it encountered one of these things. Somehow the alien presence got inside the rocket and fused with the pilot. The first we knew something had gone wrong was when the pilot turned his rocket around and headed back to Earth, ignoring all our attempts at communication. The military wanted to shoot it out of the sky, but we persuaded them that we needed to know what had happened if we were to prevent it from happening again.

'The rocket returned to our launch site in the Orkneys and crashed as much as landed. When the pilot emerged from the wreckage, he wasn't human any more.'

He broke off again, staring back into his memories.

'Had the pilot been altered into something alien?' I said.

'More like inhabited or possessed,' said Sharpe. 'And . . . he could do things.'

'Like what?' said Melody.

'Terrible things,' said Sharpe. 'It was like the whole world and everything in it was only there for him to play with. The military killed him. Just kept shooting and shooting, riddling the spacesuit with bullets, until finally he collapsed and stopped moving. And that was the end of the British Rocketry Group. They shut the whole thing down, to make sure we couldn't bring back anything else.'

'What happened to the pilot's body?' I said.

'Locked away in the Preserve,' said Sharpe. 'As a warning. I was put out to pasture, along with all my colleagues. The military wanted to shoot us, too, but the government felt there was always a chance they might need the knowledge locked away in our heads. So we were allowed to disappear into the groves of Academe, in return for our silence. And all I could do was sit and watch as the American astronauts took their first steps on the Moon, and wonder if they would trip over something we had left behind.

'And that was that . . . until three days ago, when someone working in the Preserve's security detail reached out to me. I still have a few contacts – people who remember the good old days. And this man was so scared he didn't know what else to do. It seems the Preserve is haunted by the ghost of the dead pilot. It has started wandering the Preserve in its old spacesuit, trying to find a way out.'

'What do you want us to do about it?' said Melody.

'Isn't it obvious?' said Sharpe. 'I want you to break into the Preserve and steal the ghost.'

Melody looked at him for a long moment and then turned to me. I nodded slowly.

'OK . . . That's doable. What's happening in the Preserve, right now?'

'So far, the ghost remains trapped,' said Sharpe. 'There are all kinds of safeguards and protections, but none of them were designed with human/alien ghosts in mind. There is a final failsafe – a nuclear device buried underneath the Preserve . . . And the military want to use it. The government are still making up their mind, so you have to get in there quickly while there's still time.'

'Do you have any idea what this ghost looks like?' I said.

Sharpe produced a phone from inside his jacket pocket. 'My security contact sent me this. It's a recording from a surveillance camera.'

He held out the phone, and Melody and I leaned in for a closer look. A glowing spacesuit, riddled with bullet holes, drifted through a museum packed with weird and unusual objects. It turned its helmeted head to stare at the camera, which stopped working. Sharpe put his phone away.

'Why do you want us to steal this ghost?' I said. 'Do you have a buyer? A collector, perhaps?'

'If you can get the ghost out, I think I can finally separate the pilot from the alien, and put him to rest,' said Sharpe. 'I owe him that much, for sending him into such danger in the first place.'

I looked at him narrowly. 'What about the alien?'

'Without a host, it should just disappear.'

Melody scowled at me. 'You've stolen some pretty strange stuff in your time, Gideon, but a ghost? Really?'

'Really,' I said.

'All right,' said Melody. She turned back to Sharpe. 'How much are you offering?'

'No payment, as such,' said Sharpe. 'But the Preserve is full of extremely collectable items, so feel free to help yourself to whatever takes your fancy. Some of the things on display in the Preserve could make you wealthy beyond even your wildest dreams.'

'What kind of things are we talking about?' I said.

'A mummy from the Martian Tombs,' said Sharpe. 'The preserved body of a woman who downloaded an alien AI into her mind. The Waldo Automaton – a clockwork robot designed to be remote-operated by human consciousness. The Kirlian Assassin . . .'

'I've heard of that,' I said. 'Someone separated his Kirlian aura from his body, so he could send it out to kill people on his behalf.'

'What's that doing in the Preserve?' said Melody.

'Apparently, the aura developed a mind of its own,' said Sharpe. 'Then there's the Counter Clock. A perfectly ordinary timepiece when it was installed on the Venus rocket, but after it returned, we discovered it could turn back Time. The government was very interested in that, until a particularly ambitious politician got too close. In a matter of moments, he aged backwards – into a child, a foetus, and finally something so small we could no longer see it.'

Melody smiled suddenly. 'I know collectors who would sell their soul, or someone else's, to get their hands on something like that. We are talking *never-having-to-work-again* money.'

Sharpe concentrated his cold gaze on me. 'Also, I am told you like to help people. Putting the pilot's ghost to rest would help it, and me.'

'You said the possessed pilot was dangerous,' I said. 'That it did terrible things.'

'When he was alive,' said Sharpe.

'We can't be sure it is a ghost,' I said. 'It could be some form of alien energy . . .'

'If this was easy, I wouldn't need the infamous Gideon Sable,' said Sharpe. 'Are you interested or not?'

'Oh, I'm definitely interested,' I said. 'But I still have questions. Starting with: why would the government lock away so many valuable items?'

'Because they're afraid of them,' said Sharpe. 'They're all dangerous, in their own way. The Preserve isn't just a museum; it's a prison.'

'You don't look old enough to have been head of the Group back in the fifties,' Melody said bluntly. 'Have you been messing with the Counter Clock?'

'Given how many exotic radiations I was exposed to, I'm amazed I'm still here,' Sharpe said calmly. 'But I won't last forever, and I want to right this old wrong while I still can. I need you to help me make amends, Mr Sable. But if you can't or won't do the job, please say so now, so I can find someone else. Before the military runs out of patience and hits the big red button.'

I thought about it. The job wasn't the problem; I already had several ideas about how to handle it. But there was something . . . off, about Professor Sharpe. The way he held himself so still and kept his face empty of emotion, as though he was looking out from behind a mask.

'How do you want us to deliver this ghost?' I said.

'Once you have transported it outside the Preserve – and how you do that is your business, not mine – you are to bring the ghost here, to the Gallery,' said Sharpe. 'And then you can walk away and forget you were ever involved.'

I nodded. 'Where is the Preserve?'

'Inside the Box Tunnel complex, just outside Bath.'

'Gideon?' said Melody. 'Why did you just wince?'

'Because I've heard of it,' I said.

'You know everything,' said Melody, just a bit sulkily.

'The Box Tunnel complex is a secret underground city originally set up to store and preserve everything the government thought they'd need to rebuild civilization after a nuclear exchange,' I said. 'Including a fleet of steam trains, because those could still be relied on to work after a major electromagnetic pulse.'

'They really thought we could survive a nuclear war?' said Melody.

'It was a simpler, more optimistic time,' said Sharpe.

'And this complex is still there?' said Melody.

'You know governments,' I said. 'They never throw away anything they think they might need.'

'Box Tunnel is currently being guarded by a small force of heavily armed soldiers,' said Sharpe. 'Once inside the complex, you will have to work your way past a great many booby traps and hidden defences before you can reach the Preserve.'

'Such as?' I said.

'State-of-the-art surveillance, automatic weapons systems and any number of hidden trapdoors . . . containing all kinds of nasty surprises.'

'Are you still in contact with the security man who sent you the image of the ghost?' I said.

'No,' said Sharpe. 'He's gone quiet. I hope he's all right.' He looked at me steadily. 'Will you take the job?'

'Yes,' I said. 'But I'm going to have to think about it. I know time is a factor, but I have to assemble a crew and work out a plan. I won't talk to you again until after the job is done, and only then to tell you when I'll deliver your ghost. Is that acceptable?'

'Of course,' said Sharpe. 'And allow me to wish you the very best of luck. Because you're going to need it.'

TWO

Making a Deal with the Devil
And Counting Your Fingers Afterwards

The door to the Whispering Gallery opened on its own, and, just like that, Melody and I were standing on the street outside St Giles'. The few people still out and about didn't even glance in our direction. Melody glared back at the church and then turned to me.

'How much of that do you believe?'

'Not nearly as much as Professor Sharpe thought we did,' I said. 'Oh, the Box Tunnel complex stuff is real enough, and I have heard about the Preserve before. But I don't think I trust Sharpe's motive when it comes to the ghost.'

Melody nodded quickly. 'There are a lot of unanswered questions about this job, starting with: why has the ghost only begun walking now?'

'The dead often have their own agendas,' I said. 'I think we need to talk to certain knowledgeable people and see what they can tell us.'

'But you're supposed to be the man who knows everything!'

'The devil is in the detail,' I said. 'Take the Box Tunnel complex, for example. The original underground city was revealed to the public, cleared out and shut down ages ago. Apart from the Preserve – because no one wanted to disturb some of the things inside it. But I have heard rumours that a different group has moved in, like a cuckoo occupying another bird's nest. And given how much people in our line of work love to gossip, I have to wonder why no one seems to know anything about what's going on under the hill these days.'

'The only thing the old order and the new would seem to have in common is the Preserve,' said Melody.

'Exactly,' I said. 'Could it be that the Preserve's remit has been expanded, and it's now home to rare and dangerous items from today's scientific field? Is everything we were just told nothing more than a cover to hide what's really going on?'

'I love the way your mind works around corners,' said Melody.

'It's not enough to be one step ahead,' I said. 'You have to know what you're going to do when you get there. For example, the professor was very forthcoming about the dangers of the Preserve, but he got very vague when it came to the levels of security surrounding it.'

'You think he's keeping things from us?'

'First rule of listening to the client,' I said. 'Pay extra attention to the things they don't say.'

'We have to assume the basics of the heist are true,' said Melody. 'Or we don't have anything to work with. But does Sharpe actually want us to steal the ghost, or is he planning to use us as a distraction while he goes after something else?'

'Good thinking,' I said. 'I have to say, I don't remember you being this sharp in the past, to be honest.'

'When have you ever been honest?' said Melody.

'When it profits me,' I said. I looked at her thoughtfully. 'Don't you think it's time for Annie to come back, now our audience with Sharpe is over? I could use her common sense.'

Melody glared at me. 'I told you: I've never heard of Annie. It's always been you and me, Gideon. And you are definitely going to need me to pull off this heist.'

I had to raise an eyebrow. 'And why is that?'

'You get top marks when it comes to the subtle planning,' said Melody. 'But you need someone you can rely on to get things done, while you're standing around thinking.'

And then she stopped and glanced casually around her, as though she just happened to be taking in the night.

'You do know we're being watched?'

'Of course,' I said. 'From the same shadows I used when I was watching St Giles'.'

'Shouldn't we do something about it?'

'What did you have in mind?'

'You hold their attention with some suitable small talk, while I sneak up behind them and ruin their day.'

'Really not a good idea, in this case.'

'Why not? I'm very good at sneaking.'

'Because I know who that is. And neither you nor I could take him on the best day we ever had.'

Melody studied the figure in the shadows with new interest. 'Should we make a run for it?'

'No point. He'd catch us. That's what he does.'

She looked at me sharply, alerted by something in my voice. 'Are you scared of this man, Gideon?'

'Of course,' I said. 'Any sane person would be.'

A tall, lean figure emerged from the shadows and walked unhurriedly over to join us, smiling easily, like a friend looking forward to renewing an old acquaintance. It was all I could do to stand my ground and smile calmly back at him. Never let them know you're sweating. Melody took her cue from me and nodded easily to the newcomer, while her hands closed into fists at her sides. The scariest man I knew finally came to a halt before us, and up close his smile was like a loaded gun.

'Hello, Mark,' I said steadily. 'It's been a while.'

'Hello, Gideon,' he said. 'Thanks for not running.' His voice was calm and quiet and full of a dark and deadly humour.

Mark was smartly and expensively dressed, like some city executive who just happened to be out for a stroll in the worst part of London, in the darkest part of the night. It was hard to get any real sense of what he looked like, with most of his face hidden behind such oversized sunglasses, but everything about the man made it clear he was horribly dangerous and didn't care who knew it. He nodded briefly to Melody.

'Aren't you going to introduce us, Gideon?'

'Melody Mead, this is Mark Stone,' I said. 'One of the most dangerous people I know.'

Melody looked at me. 'More than the Damned?'

'Let's just say I'd be hard-pressed on which way to bet if they ever go head to head,' I said carefully. 'Lex could break the world while he's in his armour, but Mark has an unbeatable advantage. You can't kill him because he's already dead.'

Melody studied Mark with new interest. 'So what are you – some kind of zombie?'

'I prefer the term mortally challenged,' said Mark.

'I would have gone with *morally* challenged,' I said. Because it's important to let truly scary people know that you're not intimidated, even when you are. I glanced easily at Melody, as though I just happened to be introducing her to some minor celebrity. 'Mark is known in all the worst places for being ready to do absolutely anything to get the job done. He is the government's blunt instrument of supernatural policy, always ready to hammer down any nail that stands out.' I looked thoughtfully at Mark. 'You let us see you, so we could have this conversation. Are you here to put the hard word on us?'

'Not yet,' said Mark. His voice was perfectly calm and easy. He might have been talking about the weather. 'Think of this as a friendly warning. For old times' sake.'

'You don't do friendly,' I said. 'And you certainly don't do sentiment.'

'How is it you know this person?' Melody said coldly.

'We've worked together, on occasion,' I said. 'When he needed someone to bring the subtle. All right, Mark: what's the warning?'

'It would be in your best interests not to get involved with Professor Sharpe. Let sleeping aliens lie.'

I met his gaze steadily. It felt like staring down a jungle cat that had just unsheathed its claws.

'Unfortunately, I've already agreed to do the job.'

'Ah,' said Mark. 'That is unfortunate.'

Melody picked up on the change in his tone and took a step forward. 'Don't you threaten us, coffin-dodger. Or I'll hammer a stake through your heart, fill your mouth with salt and bury you at a crossroads. And then piss on you at midnight.'

'It wouldn't help,' Mark said calmly.

'It really wouldn't,' I said. 'Let's keep this civilized, Mel.'

She ignored me, giving Mark the full glare. 'Why are you wearing shades at night?'

He smiled and pulled the sunglasses partway down his nose. His eyes were on fire, burning with a harsh crimson flame.

'All the better to see you with, my dear.'

'What the hell are you?' said Melody. Her gaze didn't waver, and her voice was as steady as ever.

Mark smiled cheerfully. 'I am the hellhound on your trail. The hunter in a world of prey. When someone goes missing from Hell, or doesn't turn up there when they're supposed to – and yes, both of those things have been known to happen – that's when I get sent to track them down and bring them back.'

'But when he's not actually working on infernal business, he'll hire out to anyone,' I said.

Mark pushed his sunglasses back into position and shrugged modestly.

'I like to keep my hand in.'

'Last I heard, you were working for one of the more obscure parts of British Security,' I said. 'How did that happen?'

'They recognize the value of a specialist,' said Mark.

'But why has British Security taken an interest in us?' Melody said bluntly.

'I don't ask questions,' said Mark. 'For me, it's all about the thrill of the chase.'

'And you always like the taste better if there's a little fresh blood in it,' I said.

Mark smiled. 'You know me so well, Gideon. Now, are you going to be a good boy and do what you're told?'

I showed him my most confident smile. 'What do you think?'

And just like that, Mark wasn't smiling any more. A sudden sense of menace hung heavily on the air, as though an unseen knife had just been pressed against my throat. I stood very still. Melody bristled dangerously.

'Don't, Mel,' I said quickly. 'Really not a good idea.'

'No one gets to speak to us like that!' said Melody. 'We have our reputations to think of! Don't just stand there; do something!'

'I already have,' I said and made myself smile coldly at Mark. 'Remember my time pen? While you were busy playing the Big I Am, I stopped Time, just long enough to slip a little something in one of your pockets. A Time Accelerator – powerful enough to age your whole body to dust in seconds. Even you'd have trouble coming back from that. So back off, or my thumb is about to get very familiar with the remote control.'

Mark looked at my right hand, buried deep in my pocket, and shrugged briefly.

'Be warned, Gideon. Stay away from Professor Sharpe. Stay away from Box Tunnel. And, above all, stay away from the Preserve. I do so hate having to go to funerals.'

He turned unhurriedly and walked away. I took Melody by the arm and hustled her down the street in the opposite direction. She tried to pull her arm free, but I just tightened my grip and kept her moving.

'We need to put some serious distance between us and the hound from Hell, Mel.'

'If he's as dangerous as you say, why haven't you already hit him with the Time Accelerator?'

'Because I made it up! By the time Mark has searched all his pockets and figured out I was bluffing, we need to be in a whole different postal area.'

I kept up the pace until we'd put several streets and a square between us and Mark, and only then did I let go of Melody's arm.

'Mark must be getting old,' I said. 'He didn't use to be that easy to fool.'

'Can the dead grow old?' said Melody. 'Anyway, given all the weird stuff you've stolen in your time, it was possible you could have something like a Time Accelerator.'

'Didn't you find it interesting,' I said, 'that Mark mentioned the Professor and the Preserve, but didn't say anything about the ghost? Perhaps he doesn't know as much about what's going on as he'd like us to think.'

'How did he find us so quickly?' said Melody.

'His masters must have been keeping an eye on Sharpe,' I said. 'Mark was probably staking out St Giles' before either of us got here.'

'We would have seen him,' said Melody.

'Not Mark,' I said. 'He's only real when he chooses to be.'

'OK . . .' said Melody. 'You are definitely freaking me out now. What is he, *really*?'

'Nobody knows,' I said. 'Some say he's a fallen angel, trying to earn his way back into Heaven. Others believe he's a sinner released from the Pit, to track down and return other lost souls. The only thing everyone is convinced of is that when the hellhound is on your trail, you're in real trouble.'

'And you worked with him,' said Melody. 'Are you friends?'

'I don't think he's allowed friends.'

Melody frowned. 'How did he know what we were talking about in the Whispering Gallery? I thought the whole point was that no one could listen in?'

'Probably just an educated guess,' I said. 'So . . . we need to put the crew back together and get to work before anyone else turns up to try to stop us.'

'Do we still need to talk to people?'

'Just the one,' I said. 'I know someone who should be able to tell us how to get into the Box Tunnel complex without being noticed.'

'The trick isn't getting in, but getting out again,' said Melody. 'With the ghost, and as much loot as we can carry.'

'No,' I said. 'The real trick is getting away with it. We have to get in and out without the authorities knowing we were ever there. So they won't have any reason to send Mark Stone after us to get their stuff back.'

'You know, we could always decline the job,' Melody said carefully. 'It's not like we signed a contract in our own blood.'

'But that's not who we are,' I said. 'We live to make the big scores, to pull off the heists no one else could manage – and stick it to the bad guys.'

'Who are the bad guys here?' said Melody.

'Given that the government is involved, I'm confident someone will make themselves known,' I said.

I set off through the early-morning streets, with Melody striding it out at my side. The few people we passed kept their heads down and avoided eye contact. Melody's patience didn't last long.

'Will Mark come after us?'

'Almost certainly,' I said. 'But not until he's consulted his masters and taken instructions. Which gives us time to quietly disappear. Mark may be hell on wheels when it comes to tracking people down, but he was never that smart. Because most of the time he doesn't need to be.'

'One problem down, and God knows how many to go,' said Melody. 'Do you have a particular destination in mind, or are we still just running away?'

'I never run away,' I said. 'I run *to*.'

'Anyone I might know?' said Melody.

'I certainly hope not. Let's just say, we're going to visit someone with expert knowledge of the Preserve.'

'So he can fill us in on all the things Professor Sharpe was keeping from us?'

'Exactly,' I said. 'People like Sharpe shouldn't even know people like us exist. And didn't it seem rather convenient to you that even though he's been out of the loop for ages, he still had a contact inside the Preserve security who could reach out to him when they had a problem?'

Melody frowned. 'Could someone be using Sharpe for reasons of their own?'

'Wouldn't surprise me,' I said. 'Still, being lied to by the client is par for the course on most heists.'

'Can you really steal a ghost?' said Melody.

'I can steal anything,' I said. 'That's pretty much my job description.'

'But have you ever done anything like this before?' said Melody. 'Do you have a ghostly butterfly net or a spiritual mouse trap?'

'Not as such,' I said.

'Have you at least worked out how we're going to break into the Box Tunnel complex?'

'Haven't a clue,' I said cheerfully. 'But I know a man who might. We are on our way to meet the Forgotten Man of British Science. Forgotten because he went to great pains to disappear so thoroughly that most people don't know he ever existed.'

'Did this man-who-never-was also screw the scientific pooch with the British Rocketry Group?'

'Oh, he was right there in the midst of it all, back in the

fifties,' I said. 'Professor Jack Jacobi – the kind of mad, crooked and bad-to-know scientist your parents warned you about.'

'OK . . . Are we nearly there yet?'

'We're here,' I said.

I gestured grandly at the sprawling structure lurking ominously ahead of us. The only illumination came from two old-fashioned street lamps at opposite ends of the street, and their light didn't travel far. Melody looked the building over and shook her head balefully.

'Not another church . . .'

'Trust me,' I said. 'This one is different. In fact, it's about as different as you can get and still be called a church.'

I drew her attention to the sign over the front door, which proclaimed in a surprisingly restrained font *The Church of Satan and All His Daemons*.

Melody looked at me. 'I am struggling to be impressed. Am I supposed to take this seriously?'

'Not in the least,' I said. 'This is Soho, after all, where the art of the con was born. Where everything is flash and flimflam, and they'll sell you the sizzle when there isn't even a steak.'

'So we're not about to walk in on a bunch of degenerate and probably very dangerous devil-worshippers?'

'Depends on how you look at it.'

'You're really not helping,' said Melody.

'I know,' I said.

'What is this place? Honestly?'

'Camouflage,' I said. 'It's all *Look away, nothing to see here, move along*. So no one will take the time to peek behind the curtain and see what's going on behind it.'

The church itself looked as though it would need a major upgrade and several coats of paint before it could qualify as drab and dull. There were no religious trimmings and nothing to indicate the nature of whatever worship was practised inside. It looked more like an abandoned warehouse.

'So the Forgotten Man of British Science . . . is in there?' Melody said finally.

'Can you think of a better hiding place?'

'And he's going to tell us everything we need to know about the Preserve?'

'Well . . .' I said. 'He might take a little persuading.'

Melody smiled. 'I can be very persuasive.'

'Let's try talking first.'

'And if that doesn't work?'

'I'll point you at him and stand well back.'

I strode up to the front door and knocked as if I had every right to. Melody tucked herself in close beside me, bouncing lightly on the balls of her feet, ready to punch out the first person who didn't show her the proper respect.

'Take it easy, take it slowly,' I said quietly. 'It's just your average devil-worshipping death cult. Nothing we can't handle.'

The door swung back before us, apparently unaided by human hand, revealing nothing but an impenetrable gloom. I strolled straight in with my head held high and Melody right beside me. The door closed behind us, cutting off the light from the street. For a moment, there was only darkness, to put us in the proper frame of mind, and then a sulphur-yellow light sprang up to illuminate a lobby packed full of huge demonic statues: the usual mix of teeth and claws and batwings, with snarling faces and hungry eyes. Mixed among them was a surprisingly eclectic mix of ancient carvings, depicting all manner of otherworldly creatures, from the blatantly threatening to the cosmically weird. Only one caught my attention . . . and I had to wonder if anyone here knew it was the real thing.

I was careful not to look at it for more than a moment and fixed my attention on the huge coloured mosaic covering the floor. A stylized devil's face stared back: the traditional curling horns, bared teeth and knowing eyes. I felt as though I should apologize for stepping on it. When I looked up, half a dozen shadowy figures had silently appeared out of nowhere to stand facing Melody and me. Long grey robes engulfed them from head to foot, with the cowls pulled forward to hide their faces. Presumably, because they thought they'd look scarier that way. They stood stiff and unmoving, like so many statues blocking our way. Melody stirred dangerously at my side, so I quickly hit the robed figures with my most confident smile.

'Hello there! Charming place you have here – very dramatic.

I am Gideon Sable, and the growling presence at my side is Melody Mead. We are here to see your glorious leader, Professor Jacobi. We aren't expected and we don't have an appointment, but I'm sure he'll see us anyway. Because the Professor and I go way back.'

'You are not welcome here,' said the figure directly in front of me. He was a good head taller than the other acolytes, and his voice was pitched ominously low.

'That is a terrific deep voice,' I said encouragingly. 'There are probably moles underground who could hear that. I couldn't get my voice that low without a third testicle. Is that your secret? Are you, in fact, hung like a pawnbroker?'

I was pretty sure I heard a couple of suppressed snickers from the other acolytes.

'The Magister doesn't like to be bothered,' said the deep voice. 'Especially by unbelievers.'

'I believe all kinds of things,' I said cheerfully. 'Starting with your leader definitely wanting to see us. That's why he opened the front door. Now be a good chap and tell his magnificence that we're here.'

'Leave,' said the acolyte. 'While you still can.'

Melody stepped forward, so she could glare right into his cowl. The acolyte didn't step back, but everyone there could tell he wanted to. Melody smiled suddenly, and not in a good way.

'One more word from you that even sounds like a threat, and I will kick you so hard between the legs that when you go to bed tonight, your balls will drop off, roll down to the end of the bed and catch fire.'

A series of low distressed noises issued from some of the other acolytes, who clearly believed every word they'd just heard.

'Let us all take a step back,' I said in my best *I'm going to be calm and civilized about this because somebody has to* voice. 'Melody, please don't frighten the nice devil-worshippers. Not until we have to.'

I reached inside my jacket, and the acolytes braced themselves, expecting some kind of weapon. Instead, I brought out my business card – the one on really good stock, with just my name on it – and handed it to the figure in front of me. He accepted the card reluctantly, as though afraid the normality might rub off on him.

'I'm going to assume you're the leader,' I said. 'On the grounds that you're the biggest, and do all the talking, and the others keep glancing at you to see what they should be doing. So – present my card to your master. And I won't tell him that you kept us waiting.'

Faced with the calm certainty in my voice, the lead acolyte turned on his heel with a dramatic swirl of his robes and disappeared through the door behind him. The other acolytes stared at me and Melody, clearly not sure what to do for the best. Devil-worshippers don't have much to fall back on once the scary fails.

Melody looked at me. 'I thought we were here to . . .'

'We are,' I said quickly. 'Not in front of the children, Mel.'

'So the head of this church is . . .'

'Oh, yes.'

'How did you get involved with the head of a coven?' said Melody.

I smiled. 'Just lucky, I guess.'

We all stood where we were and waited. None of the acolytes said anything. Perhaps because they couldn't do deep enough voices. Melody scowled at them.

'I could crush you with my thumb.'

One of the acolytes stepped forward. When she spoke, her voice was harsh and cold.

'You think you can threaten us in our own church?'

'Was that voice supposed to impress us?' said Melody. 'I've had scarier bowel movements.'

I nodded solemnly. 'It is hard to scare us. We work with the Damned.'

Some of the acolytes actually shuddered. A few made low, moaning noises. Melody looked at me.

'Do we really need this guy's help?'

'Jacobi was a pretty big name, back in the day.'

'Then how did he end up here?'

'The problem with Jack,' I said, 'was that he never met a secret he couldn't wait to sell. Eventually, inevitably, someone caught him at it, so he had to go on the run. And Mark Stone was tasked with finding him.'

'Then how is this guy still alive?'

'Jack tried being a whole bunch of different people, not always successfully. Eventually, he came to me, and I stole a whole new identity for him. Who'd look for the Forgotten Man of British Science in a setting like this?'

'Assuming he still knows useful things about the Preserve,' said Melody, 'what makes you so sure he'll tell us?'

'He owes me,' I said.

'Your faith in human nature never fails to warm my heart,' said Melody.

'And I could always tell Mark where to find him,' I said.

The lead acolyte returned, and the others looked at him with a sense of relief. They'd been listening so hard to Melody and me that they'd nearly toppled over from leaning forward.

'The Magister will see you now,' said the head acolyte.

Melody looked at me and mouthed the word *Magister*.

'The man in charge,' I said. 'Play nicely, Mel.'

She looked coldly at the robed figures before her. 'Make some room, children of the night. Or I will knock you down and walk right over you.'

The acolytes all but fell over each other in their hurry to get out of our way. The female acolyte held her ground the longest, only stepping out of Melody's way at the last possible moment. I looked at Melody and shook my head sadly.

'Can't take you anywhere . . .'

The head acolyte led us through a series of opulently appointed corridors, all of them lit with the same unhealthy yellow light. I could smell sulphur and spoiled milk and freshly spilled blood. Hell's perfume. I didn't say anything. For all I knew, it had come out of a spray can. The acolyte kept a wary eye on Melody and me, as though concerned we might steal something.

The walls were crammed with paintings depicting scenes in Hell. Horned demons tormented naked sinners, who seemed to be enjoying themselves tremendously. There were yet more statues and carvings, depicting all kinds of fantastical creatures, most of which struck me as highly unlikely. Offerings of animal guts had been laid out in bowls – so fresh they were still steaming. The smell hung heavily on the air, a very real presence in an unreal setting. Melody shot me a look.

'This is starting to feel less amusing and a great deal more devilish.'

'There's nothing here to worry about,' I said firmly. 'It's all just carnival sideshow stuff.'

And then we passed a desecrated Christian altar, with inverted crosses carved deep into the stone. The whole thing had been splashed with blood, so recently that some of it was still dripping on to the floor.

'Probably goat's blood,' I said.

'And denial's not just a river in Africa,' said Melody. 'If I see anything to convince me your friend truly has gone over to the dark side, I will burn this place to the ground and dance naked on the ashes.'

'Not until after he's told us what we need to know,' I said firmly.

Melody sniffed. 'Perfectionist.'

'Professional,' I said.

'What if he decides he's not going to answer your questions? Heads of devil-worshipping death cults aren't exactly noted for their generosity of spirit.'

'If he gives me a hard time,' I said. 'I'll give him to you.'

Melody smiled briefly. 'You're too good to me.'

'Yes,' I said. 'I am.'

Our silent guide finally brought us to a closed door with a massive pentacle carved into the wood. The acolyte knocked respectfully and then nodded to a muffled reply. He stepped to one side, and the door swung majestically back. I strode past the acolyte with my nose in the air, and Melody swept in after me.

The pleasant, comfortable room was lit by everyday electric lights, in cheerful comparison to the gloom and doom of the outer church. There were no devil-worshipping trappings, just a large business desk covered with the kind of computers you'd expect to find in any office. The Magister stood up behind the desk to greet us. A big, burly middle-aged man in a smart business suit, with a bald head and a great bushy beard, his gaze was sharp and piercing, but his smile seemed entirely genuine. He thrust a large hand across his desk, and I shook it briefly, giving him my most businesslike smile.

'Gideon, old boy!' boomed the Magister. 'So good to see you again! It has been a while, hasn't it? And this must be . . .'

'No, it isn't,' I said quickly. 'This is Melody Mead.'

Jacobi shot me a quick look and then nodded to Melody. One look in her eyes was enough to convince him not to shake her hand.

'Charmed, I'm sure.'

'Mel, allow me to present Professor Jack Jacobi,' I said. 'We go way back.'

'Old friends?' said Melody.

'Well,' I said. 'I don't know that I'd go that far . . .'

'Old friends and boon companions,' Jacobi said cheerfully.

And then he stopped and looked past me. I glanced back at the door and found it was still half open, with the hooded acolyte standing stiffly in the gap.

'Thank you, Cyril,' Jacobi said loudly. 'That will be all. You can go now.'

'I don't like leaving you alone with outsiders, Magister,' said Cyril. 'They have no respect for the church.'

'Gideon and Melody don't respect anything,' said Jacobi. 'That's the point. But I assure you, I'm perfectly safe in their company.'

'I'll leave the door ajar,' said Cyril.

He stepped back, and the door almost but not entirely closed itself.

'Probably had to become a devil-worshipper with a name like Cyril,' I said. 'I blame the parents.'

Jacobi sighed resignedly. 'My acolytes worship me. Which is, of course, right and proper and as it should be, but it's not supposed to get in the way of doing what I tell them to do. I'll have to increase their dosages again.' He sat down and gestured for me and Melody to take the comfortable chairs set out before him. He waited until we were settled and then folded his hands together on top of the desk.

'You're lucky to catch me in. I've only just returned from doing a little business.'

'Like what?' said Melody. 'Raising spirits from the vasty deep? Blighting crops and poisoning reservoirs?'

'Something like that,' said Jacobi.

I fixed him with a stern gaze. 'Don't tell me you've started to believe your own legend?'

Jacobi smiled and shook his head. 'It's not often I get to go out, these days. My followers are always ready to make sure I have anything I need. Or that they think I might want. That's the point of followers. But it's so hard to get any time to myself . . . If I didn't sneak out occasionally, I'd go crazy. Still! My position does have its perks. Would you care for some tea and biscuits?'

'Why not?' I said.

'Do you have any digestives?' said Melody. 'I do like to dunk.'

Jacobi raised his voice. 'Pot of tea for three, and the tea-time assortment, please.'

The door immediately swung open to admit a tall thin Goth girl in tight black leathers, carrying a silver tray with our order already laid out on it. She looked as though she could use a good meal or two, and her face was made up in the full Goth black and white, like an anorexic panda. She placed the tray carefully on the desk in front of Jacobi and bowed deeply. Melody and I didn't even rate a glance.

'How did she prepare that so quickly?' said Melody.

'She didn't,' I said. 'He always has tea and biscuits when he has visitors. The girl was just standing by. Right, Jack?'

He smiled unashamedly. 'You know me so well.'

'Will there be anything else?' said the Goth girl. Her voice was cold and harsh, and I immediately recognized her as the second acolyte. I wondered if they all dressed like her, under their robes.

'That will be all, Lily,' Jacobi said firmly. 'And tell Cyril I know he's still hanging around in the corridor. I can hear him breathing. If he must lurk, tell him to do it quietly.'

Lily bowed again and backed respectfully out of the room. Once again, the door almost but not quite closed itself.

'Pretty little thing, isn't she?' said Jacobi.

'Why is she dressed that way?' said Melody.

Jacobi looked at her. 'Is this a trick question?'

I stared at him coldly. 'When I set this up for you as a cover, you weren't supposed to embrace the whole Satanic panic thing.'

Jacobi shrugged. 'It's only theatre, old boy. You know I don't believe in any of this stuff.'

'But your followers do,' said Melody.

'Of course!' said Jacobi. 'That's the whole point of having acolytes. They believe, so I don't have to. And if they trust me to be what I say I am, then that's what I am. You taught me the power of belief, Gideon, when you reinvented yourself as a master thief. Just as you taught me that when a man shaves his head and grows a big beard, no one will recognize him. So . . . shall I be mother?'

I waited patiently while he poured the tea and waved for Melody and me to avail ourselves of the milk and sugar. Melody also helped herself to the biggest chocolate biscuit on the plate, and Jacobi and I pretended we hadn't noticed.

'Now then, old friend,' Jacobi said finally. 'What brings you my way?'

'I've been talking to one of your former colleagues,' I said. 'Professor Sharpe, of the British Rocketry Group.'

Jacobi looked shocked. 'He's still around?'

'Why not?' I said. 'You are.'

'But he never had the guts to do the things I did,' said Jacobi. 'What did he want with you?'

I brought him up to speed on the Preserve and the ghost, and Jacobi settled back in his chair to think about it.

'Can you do it?' he said finally.

'Please,' I said. 'Remember who you're talking to.'

Jacobi smiled briefly. 'My apologies.'

'Though it might be a little trickier than I expected,' I said. 'On the way here, I bumped into someone else we both know. Mark Stone.'

Jacobi sat up straight. 'Good God!'

I had to smile. 'Better not let your followers hear you using language like that.'

'How much does the hellhound know about what's going on?' said Jacobi.

I shrugged. 'Hard to tell, with him. But he's certainly taking an interest.'

Melody stirred uneasily. 'Is Stone really . . .?'

'Oh, yes,' Jacobi said absently.

'So he's the real deal,' said Melody. 'Unlike you.'

Jacobi didn't rise to the bait. He was too busy concentrating on me.

'Are you still contemplating going ahead with this heist?'

'Of course,' I said. 'But I could use a little assistance. What can you tell us about Professor Sharpe? You used to work with him . . .'

'Sharpe was utterly ruthless,' Jacobi said flatly. 'Always ready to sacrifice his people to achieve his own ends. Which weren't always clear.'

'Was the Rocket Group as successful as he claimed?' said Melody.

'Scientifically speaking, yes,' said Jacobi. 'Sharpe was one of the greatest minds of his generation, miles ahead of everyone else. His rockets turned outer space into our backyard . . . But the Group wasn't very good at producing by-products that could make money. Our little trips into the universe were becoming increasingly expensive, and the pressure on the Group to be self-financing was becoming overwhelming.' He stopped and frowned. 'And I always thought there was something odd about that last mission. The one that led to the Group being shut down permanently.

'It was never clear to me – to any of us – why Sharpe was so determined to send a rocket to Venus. It's not like there's anything there. I could see the sense in going to the Moon and Mars. Planetary bases – maybe even colonization, once we'd got the bugs out of the terraforming process. But Venus . . . According to all the probes we sent, it's a vicious poisonous hellhole. But Sharpe pushed the mission through over everyone's objections.

'Afterwards, I did wonder whether Sharpe knew in advance that there was a presence out there, between Earth and Venus, whether he was determined to bring back something so impressive the government wouldn't be able to justify shutting everything down. But in the end, the possessed pilot was so dangerous it put a stop to all our hopes and dreams.'

'What made him such a threat?' I said.

Jacobi stared at his hands on the desk. 'After the alien force fused with the pilot, he was no longer human.'

He paused, as though he still found it difficult to talk about. His eyes were lost in the past, just like Sharpe's.

'I was there when the Venus rocket returned to the Orkneys. The pilot should have died in the crash, but he walked unharmed out of the wreckage and the flames. People ran to help him, and that was when we discovered he could remould the shape and nature of living things, just by looking at them. He made them melt, and explode, and change . . . I saw him crush two people together, to make a single living organism that only stopped screaming when the military shot it. They were understandably terrified at the prospect of an invasion by creatures that could do things like that, so they killed the pilot. Didn't even wait for instructions – just opened fire with everything they had. The pilot didn't die easily; the thing inside kept him alive. They had to keep firing and firing until finally he hit the ground and stopped moving. The soldiers kept on firing anyway, because they needed to be sure.'

Jacobi broke off and looked at me steadily. 'And now its ghost has started haunting the Preserve. If it could do such awful things while it was alive, what will it do now it's dead?'

'How did the pilot's body end up in the Preserve?' I said.

'Where else were they going to put it?'

'Do you think the ghost can get out?' I said.

Jacobi leaned forward over his desk and lowered his voice confidentially. 'I don't think anybody knows. I still have contacts, inside the Preserve. Some of them reached out to me, but all they could say for sure was that everyone was panicking big time.'

'You still keep in touch with these people?' I said. 'After everything I went through to separate you from your old life?'

Jacobi shifted uncomfortably in his chair. 'I get nostalgic. You know how it is. But you don't have to worry. It's always done through a series of cut-outs, so no one can track me here.' He stopped and sighed slowly. 'The pilot returned to Earth in 1957. Some days that feels like another world, and sometimes it feels like yesterday.'

'You don't look old enough to have been around then,' said Melody.

'There's a reason for that,' said Jacobi. 'And I'm not going to tell you what it is.' He winked at her roguishly and shot me an arch look. 'Or you.'

I looked around his office. 'You've done well for yourself, Jack.'

'Thanks to your help in getting me started,' said Jacobi. 'And now it's time to pay the piper . . . Though, given how long I've been out of the loop, I'm not sure what I can usefully contribute.'

'You still have contacts inside the Preserve,' I said. 'You must know something about its security protocols.'

'I keep a few lines of communication open,' said Jacobi. 'In self-defence. So I'll have some advance warning for when they finally find out where I am.'

'They didn't warn you that Mark Stone had come to Soho,' said Melody.

'No,' said Jacobi, 'they didn't.' He sighed heavily and returned his attention to me. 'I can offer you a few useful passwords and security overrides, but given the Preserve's current heightened paranoia, the odds are most of them will have been changed by now.'

'I'll take them anyway,' I said. And then I looked at him thoughtfully. 'Hiding from your past is one thing, but this whole pack of apostles thing . . . What's really going on here?'

'My best-ever experiment in mind control,' said Jacobi. 'Using drugs, psychological conditioning and several very special techniques of my own devising. I wanted to see just what I could get these people to believe. How far I could push them, how extreme and even ridiculous I could make the articles of this church and still have them bow down to me. Oh, the things I've persuaded them to do . . . Always to themselves and each other, of course. Never to outsiders or innocents. When I'm done, when I've broken them all beyond any chance of a return to sanity, I shall write the

most marvellous book. Not sure where I'll get it published
. . . South America, probably.'

He took in my expression and grinned suddenly.

'Don't start feeling sorry for the acolytes. They were warped
and twisted souls long before they came knocking at my door.
I only accepted the worst of the worst for my church, because
they belonged here. You can be sure they deserve all the appalling
things I've done to them. And you needn't look at me like that,
Gideon. You always boast you only steal from people who need
punishing; how is what I'm doing any different?'

'I don't do it because I enjoy it,' I said.

Jacobi shrugged. 'You say tomato, I say job satisfaction.'
He broke off to look at me narrowly. 'I have to ask: why did
Sharpe reach out to you? Is there some new threat to the
Preserve that I haven't heard about?'

'The military are talking about blowing the whole place up,'
I said. 'Apparently, there's a nuke under the floorboards.'

'That would add a certain sense of urgency,' said Jacobi.
'And you're still prepared to go in there?'

I smiled. 'The dangers just add to the sense of adventure.
Perhaps you'd care to join us?'

Jacobi shook his head firmly. 'I have turned my back on
science. The one thing the British Rocketry Group taught us,
beyond any shadow of a doubt, is that we don't belong out there.'

'Why do you think Sharpe is so keen to get involved
again?' I said.

'Has to be the ghost,' said Jacobi. 'The last remnant of his
greatest failure. Old men have a tendency to look back over
their lives and want to atone for past sins. It's even possible
that the old fool has finally developed a conscience, though I
wouldn't put money on it.'

'What can you tell us about the contents of the Preserve?'
I said.

Jacobi smiled slowly. 'Amazing things. Incredible things.
And every single one of them locked away from the world
for really good reasons.'

'But what specific items are we talking about?' I said
patiently.

'You want names?' said Jacobi. 'How about the Karma

Cannon – a weapon that could change or corrupt a whole country's luck? It's never been used, to my knowledge. Apparently, the recoil would be devastating. Then there's the Time Storm, which was designed to slam different eras up against each other. The military killed its inventor when he threatened to demonstrate it.'

'And these things are still in the Preserve?' said Melody.

'Let's hope so,' said Jacobi.

'I know collectors who would put out serious money to get their hands on them,' I said.

'Even though they're dangerous?' said Melody.

'Because they're so dangerous,' I said. 'Collectors do love a good story, to go with their acquisitions.' I looked at Jacobi. 'Is there anything alien inside the Preserve? From the crashed starship, perhaps?'

'Just the odd Martian mummy . . . and the dead pilot's body,' said Jacobi. 'British Security has a whole different department that deals with that sort of thing.'

I nodded. 'Black Heir.'

'How do you know about them?' Melody said immediately.

'Because I get around,' I said. I concentrated on Jacobi. 'What happened to the alien ship?'

'Torn apart, gutted, sold off and used up,' said Jacobi. 'Some of it might still survive, but even when I was involved, that kind of information was way above my pay grade.' He looked at me steadily. 'Would I be right in assuming you intend to help yourself to whatever isn't nailed down, when you go after the ghost?'

'We'd be crazy not to,' I said. 'Would you like us to bring you back a souvenir?'

Jacobi shook his head firmly. 'They haven't got anything I'd want. And if you're wise, you won't touch any of it. Everything in the Preserve was buried away there for a very good reason.'

I just nodded. 'You'd better write down the passwords and overrides.'

Jacobi picked up my card from his desk and wrote quickly on it with a gold-tipped fountain pen. He passed the card back to me, and I glanced at it and put it away.

'Is there anything else you think we ought to know?' I said.

'Yes,' said Jacobi. 'Don't push your luck, Gideon. Just steal your ghost and head for the exit.'

'Understood,' I said. But I still looked at him steadily.

He sighed quietly. 'I think this falls under the heading of encouraging you in your folly, but . . . There is a way into the Box Tunnel complex that just possibly no one knows about any more. An old side entrance, dug into the earth of the hill. Back in the day, certain younger scientists would use it to sneak out and go drinking in the nearby towns. And impress science groupies.'

'That's a thing?' said Melody.

'Oh, you'd be surprised,' said Jacobi. 'Or, perhaps more properly, appalled.'

He gave precise directions on where to look. 'The door was left overgrown by design; there's no telling what it looks like now. And don't ask for the entrance codes; I never knew them.'

I just smiled. 'Locked doors have never been a problem for me.' I got to my feet, and Melody quickly joined me. 'What do I owe you, for this very helpful audience?'

'On the house,' said Jacobi. 'What are old friends for? Now, off you go. Hail, Satan!'

'I'll tell Mark you were asking after him,' I said.

When we left the office, Cyril wasn't waiting in the corridor. In fact, there was no sign of a robed acolyte anywhere. The whole church seemed ominously quiet, and it didn't help that everywhere I looked, something demonic was staring back at me. Fortunately, I'd memorized the route we'd been led through, because I always do, and Melody and I soon ended up back in the lobby. And that was when a small army of robed figures emerged from the shadows to surround us.

'There's no need for any quarrel,' I said in my most reasonable tone of voice. 'Our business is done, and we are leaving.'

'You're not going anywhere,' said Cyril in his deepest voice.

'You disrespected the Magister,' said Lily in her unmistakable voice.

'You were overly familiar,' said Cyril.

'I thought every coven leader was entitled to a familiar,' said Melody.

Lily stared at her. 'We don't find humour funny.'

'Oh, please,' I said. 'It's like you're giving her ammunition.' I made a point of addressing all the acolytes. 'Don't make this any more unpleasant than it has to be. We won't be bothering you again.'

'No,' said Lily. 'You won't.'

All the acolytes took one step forward, closing in from every side. Dozens of threatening figures with no faces, immovable in their purpose. It occurred to me that while Jacobi might know this was all just a mind game, his followers believed. And they were getting ready to prove it to us. Melody and I moved quickly to stand back to back.

'You're going to die,' said Cyril. 'We will cut the unbelief out of you and send you screaming to our Lord in Hell.'

'I don't think our very good friend the Magister would approve of that,' I said.

'He doesn't need to know,' said Cyril.

'There's no need to bother him,' said Lily.

'You'll just disappear,' said Cyril. 'And never bother anyone again.'

'I think they mean it,' I murmured over my shoulder to Melody.

'Can you use your pen?' she said just as quietly.

'I could, but we'd never force our way through this many people before we ran out of air.'

'Then you'd better get ready to guard my back,' said Melody. 'Because it's acolyte ass-kicking time.'

'Make me proud,' I said.

'Always.'

She launched herself at Cyril and punched him out. While he was falling backwards, she back-elbowed another figure in the throat, and then spun round with an outstretched leg and kicked Lily's feet out from under her. The other acolytes froze where they were, shocked by such unexpected defiance, and Melody raged among them, punching and kicking and scattering robed figures all over the place.

But they soon found their purpose again and came at her

from all sides, pressing in close so she didn't have room to manoeuvre. Some were already heading in my direction when I raised my voice.

'*Nobody move!*'

For a moment, that actually worked. They were so used to responding automatically to authority that they all crashed to a halt. I moved quickly over to stand with Melody, and the acolytes fell back to let me pass. I offered Melody my arm, and she leaned on it heavily, breathing hard.

'I could have handled this. I had them exactly where I wanted them.'

'Good to know,' I said. I looked at Cyril and Lily, who were back on their feet again. 'Get these people out of our way, or I will summon Hecate's Cat to deal with you.'

There was a pause.

'You don't have that kind of power,' said Lily.

'You really think the Magister would make time for someone who didn't?' I said.

Lily looked at Cyril. 'He's bluffing.'

'Of course he is,' said Cyril.

'Kill them,' said Lily. 'And take your time. I want to hear them beg for mercy.'

I remembered Jack telling me that everyone here had done terrible things before they came to him, that they deserved everything he did to them . . . But in the end, it was what I heard in Lily and Cyril's voices that decided me.

I aimed my skeleton key at the one truly dangerous statue I'd spotted earlier, the one carved into the likeness of a cat from hell. I turned the key and unlocked the spell that kept it sleeping, and Hecate's Cat appeared right in the midst of the acolytes. All teeth and claws and spitting fury from being imprisoned inside a statue for so long.

The huge shape tore through the acolytes with appalling speed, sending blood and severed limbs flying through the air. Cyril and Lily were the first to fall, dying a much quicker death than they'd meant for Melody and me. Screams filled the lobby but were quickly cut off, and the air was heavy with the bad coppery stench of spilled blood. The last few acolytes made a run for the door, but they never made it. Finally,

Hecate's Cat sat crouched in a welter of blood and gore, feeding messily on the bodies of its victims and ostentatiously ignoring the people who'd set it free.

'OK . . .' said Melody, keeping her voice low so as not to attract the Cat's attention. 'Is it very wrong of me that I can't find it in myself to feel bad for what happened to those people?'

'No,' I said. 'They had much worse planned for us.'

'Do you think Jacobi will be upset that we killed off his followers?'

'Not for long,' I said. 'There's never any shortage of potential disciples.'

'We're going to have to do something about that man, aren't we?' said Melody.

'Yes,' I said. 'He's not the man I remember. But first, the Preserve.'

'Any idea how we're going to get past the really big demon thing sitting between us and the door?'

Hecate's Cat turned its massive head to look at us. Blood dripped thickly from its jaws.

'Nice kitty,' I said hopefully.

It rose to its feet. I pointed the skeleton key, and although Hecate's Cat launched itself at us, it was a statue that landed at our feet.

'Bad kitty,' said Melody.

'I thought so,' I said.

'Let's get the hell out of here,' said Melody.

We walked quickly away from the church. The streets were completely deserted, and even Soho's early-morning air seemed clean and clear after the stink of blood and death in the lobby.

'Didn't it seem odd to you that Jacobi knew so much about the Preserve?' said Melody after a while.

'Given how much trouble I had to go through to separate him from his old life – definitely,' I said.

'Isn't it also just a bit odd that Sharpe and Jacobi should both have contacts inside the Preserve?'

'Well spotted,' I said. 'They know a lot more than they're telling us.'

'So . . . we are actually going to do this?' said Melody. 'Even though it involves a ghost that may not be entirely human, an army of security guards . . . and a nuke?'

'Of course,' I said. 'If half of what I've heard about the Preserve's treasures is true, I can't wait to get my hands on them.'

Melody just nodded. 'And you absolutely *can* steal a ghost?'

'If it is a ghost.'

Melody looked at me sharply. 'What else would it be?'

'That's the question, isn't it?'

Melody waited until it was clear I wasn't going to say any more, and then sighed heavily.

'Talk to me about Mark Stone.'

'I'd rather not.'

'If we really do have a hellhound on our trail . . .'

'Then we need to keep moving,' I said firmly.

We walked in silence for a while.

'We're going to need the whole crew for this,' I said finally. 'The Damned, Switch It Sally and Polly Perkins.'

And that was when Sally came striding down the street towards us.

'You have to help me, darlings! Someone's kidnapped Lex and Polly!'

THREE

Loss and Revenge
And a Really Nice Cup of Tea

For a moment, Melody and I just stood there, looking blankly at each other and then at Sally. Because there are some things you just never expect to hear.

'The Damned and the werewolf?' I said finally. 'Who could be powerful enough to take them down?'

'Are we going to have to drop everything to rescue them?'

'If need be,' I said. 'The crew is family.'

Sally finally slammed to a halt before us. She was wearing a faded leather jacket with fringed sleeves, distressed jeans and white plastic stilettos, and her dark-skinned face was gaunt with strain. She had to take a moment to get her breathing under control before she could speak.

'We can't talk here. We need somewhere private. And I have just the place in mind.'

She produced a playing card from inside her jacket pocket and held it up: the Ace of Thorns. She tossed it into the air, and the card hung there for a moment before suddenly expanding to be the size of a door. Sally gestured sharply, the door swung open, and she strode through without even glancing back. Melody and I exchanged a resigned look and went after her.

I immediately recognized the Thieves Bazaar – a great sprawling barn of a place that seemed to stretch off into the distance no matter which way you were looking. It had to be that big to fit everything in, because this was one of those places between places, where people like us go to buy the things we need to do the things we do.

Something that might have been dope smoke or the dragon's

breath curled lazily on the air, adding a helpfully concealing
haze to the various stalls, booths and pitches that packed the
Thieves Bazaar from end to end. Everywhere I looked, people
– and things that couldn't pass for people even if you closed
both eyes and banged your head against a wall – were bustling
back and forth in pursuit of the kind of deals the waking world
couldn't be allowed to know about. Because then everyone
would want their share. No one paid any attention to our
sudden appearance, because that kind of thing was just par
for the course wherever criminals, chancers and cut-throats
come to wheel and deal and cheat each other blind.

I glanced behind me. The Ace of Thorns had gone back to
being a playing card and was hanging patiently in mid-air.
Sally snapped her fingers, and the card shot back into her hand.
She tucked it carefully away in her jacket pocket, and I took
a moment to look her over.

Switch It Sally was a tall young lady with dark skin and
an aristocratic bearing, wide eyes and dyed blonde hair in a
bowl cut. Normally, she could be relied on to be the epitome
of poise and charm, a style she'd spent years cultivating as
she conned and thieved her way through the underworld of
crime. Now she looked as though someone had pulled the
world out from under her feet. But when she finally spoke,
her voice was still the same crisp cut-glass finishing-school
accent I knew for a fact she wasn't entitled to.

'Sorry for the sudden exit, darlings, but someone unusually
persistent has been dogging my high heels and I can't afford
to be caught. Not while Lex and Polly need our help.'

I decided to start with the basics. 'Sally, how did you get
your hands on a travel card?'

'The same way you would, darling. I stole it.'

I was ready to press her on that, because an inter-dimen-
sional travel card was head and shoulders above the circles
she usually moved in, but the haunted look on her face brought
me up sharp. Whatever had happened to Lex and Polly, it
wasn't just bad; it was *really* bad. Sally looked quickly around
to make sure no one was paying us any undue attention, which
only went to show how rattled she was. One of the few
unbreakable rules in the Thieves Bazaar is that everyone minds

their own business. Sally stepped in close and lowered her voice.

'We have to rescue Lex and Polly. Before it's too late.'

'Are they here?' I said.

'What? No, of course not!'

'Then why bring us to this den of thieves?' said Melody.

'Because it's so packed and noisy here we can be sure no one will overhear us. Because no one could hope to follow us through the Bazaar without being noticed. And because if you upset the security here, it will eat you alive. Now, please, follow me, darlings.'

She hurried off through stalls and booths selling everything from illegal tools of the trade to weapons for every criminal occasion, and Melody and I followed after her. We don't normally allow Sally to take the lead, because it nearly always ends with the rest of us up to our knees in trouble, but the wounded look on her face was a powerful persuader.

I paused before some of the stalls, just in case there was something I could use. Most of the stuff on display was the usual criminal flotsam and jetsam. Portable doors – dark pliable blobs that, once you slapped them against a wall, would become a door that could take you anywhere. False faces for when you needed to be someone else in a hurry. Even a few seven-league boots for repeated short-range tele-ports, when the people coming after you turned out to be really determined. Along with treasures and trinkets from every part of the world, with nothing even remotely like a provenance or a guarantee.

Scarecrows dressed as Pierrots and Columbines leaned casu-ally against their wooden crosses, all ragged silks and painted faces. They watched everyone and everything with their blank eyes, just waiting for an excuse to leap into action and admin-ister beatings. They were the Bazaar's enforcers, programmed to react to even a hint of a pickpocket in action, the beginnings of a brawl or someone who didn't belong. All the scarecrow heads turned slowly to watch me pass, but none of them moved away from their crosses.

Everyone we encountered seemed to know Sally, and she managed a charming smile and a cheerful word for all of them, because that was how she operated. Even in the midst of a crisis, she was still the consummate professional. And, of course, she didn't want anyone to know she was in trouble because that might make her appear vulnerable, and the Thieves Bazaar has always reacted badly to the scent of blood in the water. Perhaps only someone who knew her as well as I did could see how much the performance was taking out of her.

Many people knew me well enough to nod respectfully, but no one seemed to recognize Melody Mead, girl adventurer. Her frown deepened into a dangerous scowl, and the people we passed gave her even more room than normal.

Sally finally came to a halt before a battered wooden door that stood alone and unsupported. The sign above read: *Ye Elven Tea Room. Founded before you were even thought of.* I sighed inwardly.

'Do we have time for a tea break? I thought this was an emergency?'

'It is,' said Sally.

'Then why bring us here?'

'The tea is excellent,' said Sally.

I considered the paint-peeling door and the handwritten sign. 'It would have to be.'

I was doing my best to be supportive, because I could see the distress running through Sally, and because I needed to know what had happened to Lex and Polly. If there was someone out there powerful enough to take them off the board, I wanted to know as much about them as possible. If only because, at some point, they might come looking for me.

Sally walked right at the door, and it swung back before her as though doing her a favour.

The tea room turned out to be big enough to hold a wedding reception for two major crime families, with enough space left over for a decent-sized floor show. Various fey and delicate touches tried valiantly for style and character but didn't even get close. Two giant aspidistras in pots were fighting over which of them got to eat a small rodent; two violins and a cello were playing minor hits from the sixties without the need for any musicians; and the views through the windows kept changing. The closely packed tables were covered with cloths that had been starched to within an inch of their lives, the straight-backed chairs were a triumph of style over comfort, and the whole place had an atmosphere of genteel decline.

An elf waitress approached, wearing a traditional French maid's uniform: all crisp black and white, with far more lace than could possibly be justified. As though the elf had been informed of the necessity for a uniform and then stabbed a finger at the wrong page in the catalogue. She tottered up to us on unfeasibly high heels and lurched to a halt. Anyone else would have broken an ankle. She had a sharp-boned face under silver hair, pointed ears and inhumanly bright eyes. She glowered impartially at all of us.

'What do you want?'

'Table for three please, dear,' said Sally.

The elf waitress spun round with almost serpentine grace and headed for a nearby table, leaving it up to us whether we followed her or not. The clatter of her heels on the marble floor sounded like a typewriter on amphetamines. She waved a hand at the table, with an air of *Take it or leave it and see if I care*, and the three of us immediately arranged the chairs so we could sit with our backs to the wall while maintaining a clear view of the entire tea room. Because we were, after all, professionals. The elf waitress smirked knowingly.

'Pot of tea for three, please,' said Sally.

'Stay there,' said the elf waitress. 'Don't move, don't feed the plants, and don't spit on the floor. I suppose you want milk and sugar as well? Thought so . . .'

She made it sound as though that was the last straw, before turning her back on us and clattering away.

'You have to be careful what you order here,' Sally said wisely. 'Above all, never ask for fairy cakes.'

I nodded solemnly. 'I can honestly say the thought had never entered my mind.'

Melody and I looked expectantly at Sally, but she just sat stiffly in her chair, staring at the pristine tablecloth. It was clear she had no intention of discussing anything until we all had a cup of tea in our hands. Perhaps because everyone knows hot sweet tea is good for shock. She must have felt the pressure of our gaze because her head came up and she smiled bravely.

'I know, darlings; but please be patient. I need to tell you what's happened, but once I start, I won't be able to stop. As bad as you think it's going to be, I promise you . . . it's going to be worse.'

I did my best to look understanding. Given some of the weird and horrific dangers we'd been through together, I was intrigued that she thought her story would disturb us. Whatever had reduced the infamous Switch It Sally to such a state had to be something way out on the far edge of the curve. To give her some breathing space, I ostentatiously turned away to study our surroundings.

Most of the other customers were elves. Dozens of the tall and slender creatures, inhumanly elegant and borderline psychotic, dressed in clothes and costumes from any number of different periods of history. The elves have been around for a very long time. Some were wrapped in thorns that stirred restlessly, as though waiting for something to attack. Others had copper and brass piercings, in locations that would have seriously distressed anything human. A few had semi-transparent heavily veined wings that had already sheared off the backs of the chairs they were sitting on.

The elves sipped their tea with practised grace and chatted quietly in a variety of languages. There was something about them that suggested children playing at being adults, holding a tea party because that was what people did. Pretending to be part of a ceremony they were ill-equipped to appreciate, just for the fun of it.

So many elves made it clear this was no place for tourists. Unless they liked living dangerously. I mentally measured the distance to the door and made sure there was nothing in the aisles that might get in the way if I felt a sudden need to race for the exit.

A few of the patrons weren't elves. The ghost of a flapper from the 1920s sat hovering a few inches above her chair, savouring the memory of tea from an empty cup. An alien Grey in the tattered remains of an ancient atmosphere suit was sipping his tea with a single extra-long finger properly extended. And one of Baron Frankenstein's less successful creations sat slumped in her chair, picking moodily at the stitches in her wrist.

None of them paid us any attention.

The elf waitress returned in a hammering of high heels, bearing a cheap tin tray with a delicate china teapot covered in hand-painted flowers of a kind not normally known in nature; three equally delicate china cups with handles so thin they were little more than a suggestion; a disreputable-looking Toby Jug for the milk; and a chunky glass bowl for the sugar, the surface of which boasted a tiny but perfect crop circle. The elf waitress slammed the tray down on our table with such force the china clattered together for support.

'Call if you want anything else.' She made it sound like a challenge.

'This will do nicely, dear,' said Sally.

The elf waitress produced a bark of sarcastic laughter and strode off. Sally reached for the teapot and showed Melody and me a smile with very little humour in it.

'Shall I be mother?'

'By all means,' I said. 'I wouldn't dare. What kind of tea is it?'

'Whatever kind you want,' she said. She poured a deadly dark mixture into her cup, and it heaved and seethed threateningly before settling. 'This is a Hy-Brasil blend. I know you only drink Tetley's, Gideon.' She poured some into my cup, and the familiar scent came curling up. Sally looked at Melody, who smiled sweetly.

'Green Monkey.'

What appeared in Melody's cup was undeniably green and looked strong enough to fight its corner. The milk and sugar proved reassuringly normal. We all sipped our tea and made the proper appropriate noises, and then I fixed Sally with a supportive but demanding look.

'Talk to us, Sally. Tell us what happened to the fiercest werewolf and the most ruthless man I have ever known.'

Sally gripped her cup with both hands and drank half her tea down in great gulps, apparently not in the least bothered by the thick steam coming off it.

'They've put Lex in a cage,' she said. 'And Polly. They're going to auction them off to the highest bidder.'

'How is that even possible?' said Melody.

Sally looked at her and then at me. 'I'm sorry, but . . . Who is this? I mean, yes, I can tell it's Annie, but . . .'

'This is Melody Mead,' I said carefully. 'Girl adventurer. Don't ask; it's complicated. Just start at the beginning and talk us through this.'

Sally shot Melody a distrustful look, placed her cup carefully on its saucer and clasped her shaking hands together.

'Polly Perkins has been like a daughter to Lex and me, ever since the Siren Song caper. The two of them dote on each other. It's been harder for me, because Polly and I have known each other for ages and fought it out over more than one big score. We get on a lot better now we aren't competing, but I think it's fair to say the role of stepmother has not come easily to me.' Sally stopped and sighed briefly. 'We were doing so well . . . until Polly decided she needed to prove herself to Lex. That she could be an adventurer and a force for the Good, just like him. So she went looking for a really bad guy to take down. And, for my sins, I encouraged her. It meant so much to her, and, after all, she is a werewolf. What trouble could she get into, that her powers couldn't get her out of?

'As one of the most celebrated exotic dancers on the scene today, Polly could get into any nightclub she fancied. All she had to do was dance, and the punters would come streaming in to worship at her feet and learn the latest moves. And so she went from club to club, through all the darkest parts of Soho – not actually getting involved in anything, just keeping her eyes and ears open. Searching for someone so bad Lex would have to be impressed when she brought the hammer down.

'She finally phoned me from a club, excited that she'd found someone so bad they deserved everything that was coming to them. I pressed Polly for his name, but she didn't want my help or Lex's. It was important to her to do this on her own. She promised she'd ring later, when it was over.

'But she didn't. I waited all evening. Lex was out on business, and he refuses to carry a phone because he doesn't want

to be bothered while he's working.' She paused, frowning.
'He's been spending a lot of time on his own since he killed
so many people while he was searching for me after I was
kidnapped. I still feel a bit guilty: that I was responsible for
sending him back to his bad old ways, after he'd made such
an effort to redeem himself and save his soul from Hell. I
really thought he could do it . . . But he threw it all away, to
save me.'

She stopped again, and when she didn't resume, I pushed
her a little.

'I didn't know you did guilt, Sally.'

She smiled quickly. 'Neither did I, darling. It came as the
most awful shock. Anyway, Lex finally came home, and I told
him what Polly had said. We still couldn't believe she might
be in any real danger. And then the phone rang. And this heavy,
gloating voice said he'd locked Polly up in a cage, like the
animal she was. For sticking her nose into things that were
none of her business. She was to be auctioned off to the highest
bidder, because there were a lot of people interested in
acquiring their very own werewolf. For her shape-changing
ability, her healing skills . . . or just for her fur. Lex was invited
to attend the auction and win Polly back by out-bidding
everyone else. With money . . . or the promise of his services.

'I'd never seen Lex's face so cold. He said if Polly was
hurt, he would unleash the horror of the Damned on everyone
involved. But the voice just laughed at him.'

She took a moment, to get her breathing under control.
Melody looked at me.

'Who would be crazy enough to get the Damned mad at
them?' And then she broke off as she saw something in my
face. 'You know who she's talking about, don't you?'

'There's only one man it could be,' I said.

'The hellhound?' said Melody.

'No,' I said. 'He wouldn't lower himself to threats. This is
a more human menace, a dark shadow from my past.'

'Lex said he was going to the club, to rescue Polly,' said
Sally. 'He wouldn't let me go with him. He said he had to do
this on his own, to send a message to anyone who thought
they could attack him through his family, but I think he just

didn't want me to see all the awful things he was planning to do. Like I would have given a damn.'

She stared at me defiantly. 'I knew who and what Lex was when I first took up with him. The man with no conscience and no restraint, because he was Damned. But still determined to do good, to spite Hell. I knew what kind of man he was when I married him. So I couldn't force myself on him if he was determined to go alone. He had his pride.

'I stayed at home and waited. And waited. Until the phone rang again, and the same voice said he'd put Lex in a cage right next to Polly's. That Lex was also up for auction, because a lot of people would be happy to get their hands on the Damned, now he'd been properly humbled and broken. People interested in justice or revenge, or just bragging rights.

'The voice on the phone sounded so happy, so arrogant, relishing all the awful things he was saying. He said to come to the club and see Lex and Polly. I wanted proof they were alive first. He laughed and said, "Of course." There was a pause, and then I heard Polly scream as if she was being skinned alive. I didn't hear Lex, and that scared me even more. What state could he be in, that they couldn't even make him cry out?

'The voice said I could bid on Polly and Lex, and pay with money or services from the master thief Gideon Sable. Oh, yes, he knew all about you – and the crew. I put the phone down on him. I wanted to go straight to the club . . . But I knew they were only waiting for a chance to put me in a cage as well, so they could use me to get at you, Gideon.'

Melody looked at me. 'Why would they want you so badly?'

'Because I can steal things no one else can,' I said. 'They must believe I'd do anything to get Lex and Polly back.'

'Well, wouldn't you?' said Sally.

'Only if all my rescue plans failed,' I said. 'And my plans never fail.'

Sally shook her head angrily. 'You have the same look on your face that Lex had, before he left. So confident, so arrogant. As though you can't possibly screw up. Well, Polly and Lex thought that, and now they're locked up in cages!'

'What happened next?' I said.

'I tried to phone you! But you had your phone turned off!' She glared at me accusingly. I met her gaze steadily.

'Mel and I must have been inside the Whispering Gallery and cut off from the world. I'll explain later.'

'I went to the shop, looking for you,' said Sally. 'You weren't there, but Sidney the talking mirror was. He said you hadn't told him where you were going. He sounded a bit put out about that. I think he gets lonely on his own. Anyway, he searched London with his all-seeing gaze and was able to pin down the point where you dropped off the map.' She looked at me sharply. 'Why didn't you tell Sidney where you were going? Don't you trust your own mirror?'

'Some things are best not spoken out loud,' I said carefully. 'Because you never know what might be listening.'

I didn't look at the elves taking their tea around us. I didn't need to.

'I decided to go to the club on my own,' said Sally. 'Not to rescue Lex and Polly, necessarily, but to see if things were as bad as they sounded. There was always the chance I could throw a spanner in the bad guy's works, or hit him over the head with it. I was pretty sure I could get in and out of the club without being noticed. One of the reasons I put so much work into looking distinctive is so no one will recognize me when I'm not.'

She nodded apologetically to Melody. 'I raided your wardrobe for this disguise. Then all I had to do was slouch and look awkward, and when I looked in the mirror, I didn't recognize myself. Sidney wanted me to wait until you got back, Gideon, because you're so good with plans, and I'm famously not. But I had no idea how long you might be . . . And not knowing what had happened to Lex and Polly was driving me crazy. So I went to the club.

'It was a bad part of town, with bad people and trouble on the air. It didn't take me long to realize this was the kind of club you ended up at when you'd been thrown out of everywhere else. A crowd was milling around outside, and there was a feeling a fight could break out at any moment. I put on my best *I am poor but incredibly violent so there is absolutely no point in messing with me* face, and no one even looked at me. They had bigger fish to slaughter.

'Security at the club door was two big men with muscles, in ugly suits that fitted where they touched. I saw one poor fool push his luck with them; when the bouncers had finished, someone had to come out with a hose to wash the blood off the pavement. I soon worked out you could only get in with a membership card, so I eased in behind someone as they approached the bouncers, and quietly switched their card for one of the many blank ones I keep about my person. Then all I had to do was flash my new card at the muscle, and they waved me on while the original owner was still searching through his pockets.'

Sally shuddered suddenly, and I felt the hackles rise on the back of my neck. Switch It Sally was a hard case, who'd learned her trade in a hard world. So whatever she'd found inside was going to be really bad. She gulped down some more of her tea, and it seemed to steady her.

'The club was awful,' she said quietly. 'I've been around, seen my fair share of sin and depravity, and enjoyed most of it . . . But this was just horrid. It wasn't a sex club, as such, more the kind of place where you could do anything to anyone, as long as you had the money to pay for it. There was blood on the walls and floor, and it was hard to tell the screams from the laughter.

'I wandered around, sticking to the edges of things, keeping my eyes and ears open. I had to punch a few men and kick one woman where it hurt, but no one pushed too hard. Because there was always someone who wanted it. It didn't take me long to understand the main club was for everyday sins and ordinary horrors. Nothing so extreme you couldn't walk away from it. The real action was going on downstairs.

'There was a door at the back of the club, tucked away in the shadows where it belonged. Security was one man, dressed like an undertaker, right down to the tails and top hat. He had a dead face and eyes that had seen everything. I walked up to him like it was no big deal and flashed him my card, and he just opened the door and waved me through.

'I made my way down a set of creaking wooden stairs, and

it felt like passing the point of no return. My skin crawled, and I had to bite down hard to keep my teeth from chattering. You know I don't scare easy, Gideon; I've faced down all kinds of bad guys in my time and laughed in their faces. This was different.

'Upstairs was bad, but downstairs was vile. The things those people were doing to each other . . . It had gone beyond sex and violence, and into the destruction of what makes people people. I had to fight to keep my face calm, and just stroll through Hell as though I'd seen it all before. Finally, I found them. Lex and Polly had been locked up in separate cages. Polly was in her human form, and Lex was unconscious. Because someone had beaten him to a pulp.'

'But he's the Damned!' said Melody. 'No one can hurt Lex while he's in his armour!'

'I know,' said Sally, with a kind of despairing calm. 'I stayed well back, trying not to make my interest in Lex and Polly too obvious. And because I didn't trust what I might do if I got too close. I'm a thief, not a fighter; but right then I could have killed everyone in that room. Oh, Gideon, there was so much blood dripping out of Lex's cage . . . Someone had tried to cut off his halos and made a real mess of his wrists. His face was so damaged it didn't even look like him any more. And someone had cut out his eyes. He was still alive. I could see him breathing.'

'What state was Polly in?' said Melody.

Sally managed a small smile. 'Oh, she was mad as hell and spitting fury. I don't know if they beat her as well; if so, her werewolf side had healed her. She was stark naked, with a silver collar around her throat and a chain fastening her to the bars. The silver hurt Polly where it touched her, but she never made a sound. People crowded around the cage, laughing and taunting her. One man boasted he was ready to pay whatever it took to buy some quality time with Polly, before the auction. But he made the mistake of getting too close to the bars, and a clawed hand shot out and ripped his face off. The people watching thought that was hilarious.

'Even a partial transformation while wearing the silver collar was enough to send Polly into convulsions. She thrashed about her cage, slamming against the bars and howling with pain, and when she was finally able to regain control of herself, she was breathing heavily, with sweat dripping off her face. She sat down hard and hugged her knees to her chest, ignoring everyone. Staring steadily at Lex in his cage, as though willing him to wake up. But he didn't.

'I started edging closer to the cages. I thought I could switch out the door locks and maybe even the silver collar. If Polly could get out and go full wolf, I could take advantage of the chaos to get Lex out, and then . . . I don't know. I wasn't thinking too clearly at that point.

'But then someone in the crowd shouted my name.' Sally smiled tiredly. 'I suppose I am quite well known in certain circles, darlings. Anyway, people started pointing at me and shouting for security. Half a dozen big guys came charging through the crowd, and since they didn't look like people I could charm into seeing things my way, I waited till they were close enough and then switched the valves in their hearts for bits of their kidneys. They were all dead before they hit the floor.'

She smiled, remembering. I was shocked. I'd known Sally to bring all kinds of dirty to a fight, but I'd never known her to kill anyone.

'I pointed my left hand at the crowd,' said Sally. 'And shouted I had a killing bone. Everyone fell back and I ran for the stairs. I didn't feel at all bad about what I'd done to the security guys. Not after everything I'd seen. I raced up the stairs and burst out into the main club. The man in the undertaker's outfit was waiting for me, so I kneed him in the nuts and rabbit-punched him as he bent over. Everyone else ignored me – too caught up in their own pleasures to care about anything else.

'I'd almost reached the main door when the club's owner called out to me. "Come back when you're ready to bid, Sally. You've got until midnight. Let the world know what I've done, that no one else has dared to do. Make them jealous, Switch It Sally." And then he laughed and laughed and laughed.

'I ran out of the door and down the street and kept on running. Until finally I had to stop because I couldn't get my breath. I bent right over, sweat dripping from my face into the gutter, along with the tears.' She smiled briefly. 'I must have looked a hell of a sight. Eventually, I phoned Sidney, and he told me where to find you.'

'We must have left the Whispering Gallery by then,' I said.

'I can't go back to the club without you,' Sally said flatly. 'But we have to go. Lex needs you. Polly needs you.'

'We'll get them out,' I said. 'No one messes with me and mine. But Sally . . . you haven't said the name yet. I need to be sure about who's behind this. Tell me the name of the nightclub owner.'

'Hogge,' said Sally. 'His name is Hogge.'

'Of course,' I said. 'It would have to be.'

There must have been something in my voice because Melody looked at me sharply.

'You two have history?'

'I know him, and he knows me,' I said. 'You didn't escape from that club, Sally; he let you go. Because he wanted you to find me and lead me back to him. This whole thing is a trap.'

'At least we've got till midnight to think about this,' said Melody. 'Time to plan some serious retributions.'

'So you are going?' said Sally.

Melody smiled suddenly. 'Of course. Lex and Polly are family.'

'Even though you know it's a trap?'

Melody shrugged. 'We know all there is to know about traps.'

Sally concentrated on me. 'How did you know it was Hogge?'

'It had to be him,' I said. 'No one else would dare. He knows I'll come because we go way back.'

'And yet you never mentioned him to me before,' said Melody.

'There are parts of my past I prefer not to remember,' I said. 'Long before I became Gideon Sable, I used to work for Hogge. He was still on his way up then, intent on making a name for himself. Hogge started as a nickname – it was said he always had his face buried in a trough. But he took the name for his own and embraced it.'

Sally stared at me. 'And you worked for him?'

'The person I was then doesn't exist any more,' I said. 'That ambitious, hopelessly naïve young man. I worked for Hogge as his accountant. All the time dreaming of a better, more glamorous life. But I couldn't keep my head in the sand forever. I found out where the money was coming from, and all the things Hogge did to get it. He taught me that actions have consequences, and crimes have victims.

'I wanted to hurt Hogge the way he hurt other people. Make him pay. By the time I'd finished doctoring his books, I'd robbed Hogge of everything except his underwear, and I was off and gone long before his pet thugs came looking. That's when I started being other people. Partly to make sure I couldn't be found, but mostly because I didn't like the man I used to be.'

'What's Hogge like?' said Melody.

'A complete and utter scumbag,' I said. 'He made his fortune out of other people's suffering and enjoyed every moment of it. He has a finger in every criminal pie, and every villain in Soho bows down to him.'

'And he's powerful enough to take down the Damned?' said Melody.

'Not personally,' I said. 'But he always has powerful people working for him. I suppose it was inevitable that at some point he'd find someone worse than the Damned. Ordinarily, I'd come up with some fiendishly clever plan, but since I have no idea who's involved or what they can do, we're just going to have to wing it. Finish your tea, ladies. We're going to Hogge's club.'

'How can we rescue Lex and Polly without a plan?' said Sally. 'That's why I came to you: because you're always the man with the plan!'

'Not this time,' I said. 'Oh, I've already worked out how to get into Hogge's club, but just bringing the sneaky isn't going to be enough this time. Hogge never gives up anything that's his. Either you pay his price or you take it from him by force. And if you do that, he'll never stop coming after you.'

'So what are we going to do?' said Sally.

I looked at Melody. 'The heist can wait.'

Melody nodded quickly. 'All for one, and vengeance for all.'

'There's no way we could raise enough money to be sure of winning the auction,' I said carefully. 'And I can't think of anything in the shop that Hogge would accept in exchange. He set all of this up to suck me in, so he can own me again.'

'You think this is all about you?' said Sally.

'Yes,' I said. 'He wants me back, because I'm the one who got away. He expects me to sacrifice myself to save Lex and Polly.'

'And would you?' said Sally.

'If I have to.' I thought for a moment. 'We're going to have to negotiate. Offer Hogge something he wants more than he wants Polly and Lex.'

'Like what?' said Melody.

'I have something in mind.'

Sally smiled suddenly. 'You do have a plan!'

'I might,' I said.

'A deal where Hogge ends up screwed?' said Melody.

'Of course,' I said.

And that was when Sally looked out over the Elven Tea Room and said, very quietly, 'Oh, shit.'

I turned quickly and there was Mark Stone, standing at his ease as he looked round the crowded room.

'How did he find us here?' said Melody.

'It's what he does,' I said. 'There's no hiding from a hell-hound. But why is he so intent on stalking us?'

'Why don't I go and ask him?' said Melody.

She started to get to her feet, but I grabbed her arm and hauled her back down again. She jerked her arm free and glared at me fiercely.

'You do that one more time and I will punch your head through a wall! What is wrong with you?'

'I just saved your life,' I said flatly. 'If Mark sees you as a threat, he'll kill you. Simple as that.'

Melody looked at Mark with new interest. 'Really? He's that dangerous?'

'Are you kidding?' said Sally. 'Everyone's heard about

Hell's hound. They say no one can stop him, hurt him or turn him aside, because the worst thing that could happen to him has already happened.'

'We can't fight him,' I said. 'So we'll just have to out-think him.'

'We're doomed,' said Sally.

I raised a hand to attract Mark's attention and gestured for him to come and join us. He peered at us over his sunglasses, and there was a brief flash of bloodred flames. He weaved calmly between the closely packed tables, and none of the other customers so much as glanced at him. He took a chair from a nearby table, set it facing us and sat down.

'Well,' he said. 'Isn't this nice?'

'How did you find us?' I said politely.

'I can find anybody,' said Mark.

'But why did you need to find us?' I said.

Mark just smiled his easy smile. 'You really should have taken the warning, Gideon.'

'I don't do warnings,' I said. 'You know that.'

Mark shook his head. 'Nevertheless . . .'

'We're not going to the Preserve,' I said carefully. 'We have to rescue Polly Perkins and the Damned from Hogge.' Mark couldn't keep from raising an eyebrow, and I sensed an opportunity. 'Perhaps you'd care to join us . . .'

'I am tempted,' said Mark. 'If only to discover how Hogge was able to capture the Damned. But I'm afraid I must decline. I have my orders.'

He didn't need to raise his voice. The threat was right there in plain sight.

I looked at him steadily. 'You sure you want to do this, Mark? You really have no idea what I can do, these days.'

'I've heard about your toys,' said Mark. 'You must know there's nothing in this world that can prevent me from carrying out my mission.'

'Because you're dead?' said Melody.

'Exactly,' said Mark.

'There are worse things than death,' I said.

'I know,' said Mark. And something in the cold certainty in his voice froze me in my chair. Mark smiled, just a bit sadly. 'It's all about duty, you see. Nothing can be allowed to get in the way of that.'

'You want to bet?' said Sally.

There was something in the way she said it that made all of us turn to look at her. She was smiling sweetly at Mark, and I felt like wincing. Sally only did that when she had something really nasty up her sleeve.

'Maybe you can't be stopped,' she said. 'But I can keep you occupied, while we leave. And remember: you brought this on yourself, Mark.' She turned her smile on me. 'I told you I had a feeling someone was coming after me. Did you think I chose this place at random?' Her gaze snapped back to Mark. 'Lex needs me. Polly needs me. And you should have known better than to get between me and my family.'

She rose suddenly to her feet, and Melody and I scrambled up out of our seats to join her. Sally raised her voice.

'*Hey, Rube!*'

And just like that, every single elf sitting at a table rose to their feet and turned to look at Sally. The few customers who weren't elves decided it was time to be somewhere else. The ghost girl blinked out of existence so quickly that the teacup she was holding fell out of mid-air, while Frankenstein's creation and the alien Grey hid under their tables. Sally smiled coldly at Mark as he rose unhurriedly to his feet. All the elves smiled at Mark, and suddenly their mouths were full of pointed teeth. Sally pointed at Mark, and when she spoke, her voice held an awful judgement.

'*Troublemaker!*'

She sprinted for the door, with me and Melody right behind her. Mark had only just started to react when every elf in the tea room surged forward and fell on him like a pack of piranhas. They swarmed all over him, slamming him to the floor by sheer weight of numbers, and then their teeth went to work. I paused briefly to look back at the heaving mass of bodies, and what I saw was enough to hurry me out the door.

Back in the Thieves Bazaar, Sally set off through the crowds at a determined pace, leaving me and Melody to play catch-up. Melody shot me a seriously freaked-out glance.

'Can even Mark Stone survive something like that?'

'I've known him come back from worse,' I said. 'But what those elves were doing to him should buy us some time.'

'He really isn't going to be pleased with us, is he?' said Melody.

'Three guesses whether I give a damn,' said Sally, not looking around. 'And the first two don't count.'

We hurried on through the Thieves Bazaar, and something in our faces made everyone else hurry to get out of our way. I moved in beside Sally.

'How did you know the elves would answer your call?'

'My mother's mother was an elf,' said Sally.

Melody nodded. 'Suddenly, much becomes clear.'

FOUR
All Kinds of Vengeance

We made our way back through the Thieves Bazaar, and everything seemed calm and peaceful – or, at least, as calm and peaceful as things ever got – because no one had any idea of what had just happened. I hurried Melody and Sally along, setting a brisk pace and trying not to look as though we were running away from something. The crowds were as dense as ever, and far too preoccupied with their own unlawful businesses to pay us any attention. Some of the scarecrows did stir uneasily on their crosses, as though they could sense something in the air. Melody scowled around her and then focused on me.

'What's the rush? We took care of Mark . . .'

'Did we?' I said.

'You honestly think he can fight off a whole pack of elves?' said Sally.

'We are talking about the hound from Hell,' I said. 'A famously unstoppable force.'

'Oh, come on, darling,' said Sally. 'Those elves had their eating trousers on. They won't stop till they've chewed up every last bit of gristle. Even Mark Stone will have trouble coming back from a series of elven bowel movements.'

Screams rang out behind us, followed by shouts and alarms and all the other sounds of fear. I crashed to a halt so quickly that Sally and Melody carried on for a few steps. Back the way we'd come, an awful lot of people were shouting and panicking and running in all directions. Some hid behind the booths and stalls, while others simply vanished in unexpected ways.

'Oh no . . .' said Sally.

'It can't be . . .' said Melody.

'It's him,' I said.

Mark Stone came striding through the Thieves Bazaar like a hound who'd caught the scent. His clothes were in tatters, but he was completely unharmed. He wasn't wearing his sunglasses, because he wanted everyone to see his burning eyes. Stalls and booths burst into flames as he walked past them, leaving a trail of burning wreckage in his wake.

'Now that's just showing off,' I said.

'He does look very upset,' said Sally.

'What are we going to do?' said Melody.

'Run,' I said.

We sprinted through the Bazaar, and the people ahead of us scattered like frightened birds. I glanced back over my shoulder, to see Mark already closing the gap between us. He wasn't so much running as forcing his way through the world by sheer strength of will. Untiring, implacable, unstoppable: the hound from Hell, in a really bad mood.

Scarecrows dropped from their crosses and hit the ground running. Dozens of Pierrots and Columbines headed straight for Mark, surging forward with boneless grace, their shabby silks flapping. They weren't scared of Mark because they didn't have the brains for it. Gloved hands reached out, to rend and tear. Mark waited till they were almost upon him and then looked at them with his burning gaze. Every single scarecrow burst into flames and was consumed in a moment, leaving nothing but ashes floating on the air.

One of the larger booths made the mistake of being in Mark's way, and he walked right through it. The whole booth exploded, and the sheer force of the blast picked up Melody and Sally and me and sent us sprawling on the hard ground. I forced myself back on to my feet, just in time to see Mark walk out of the roiling cloud where the booth had been. I hauled Melody and Sally up and got them moving again, and together we ran for our lives.

We were all bruised and shaken and breathing hard, but we couldn't let that slow us down. Our feet pounded painfully on the bare stone floor. At least there was no one left to get in our way. Everyone else had already left the building, or dived into a hole and pulled it in after them.

'I can't believe he got away from that many elves,' said Sally.

'This is a man who's done time in Hell,' I said. 'All you did was make him angry.'

'I didn't see *you* doing anything!' said Sally.

'I was still hoping I could reason with him.'

'Good luck with that now,' said Melody.

Sally glared at me. 'Think, Gideon! There must be something you can do!'

'I'm doing it,' I said.

'What about the time pen?' said Melody.

I stumbled to a halt and took out the pen. It felt good to have a good excuse to stop. The others stopped with me, breathing hard.

'Grab hold of my shoulders,' I said. 'And make sure you get a good grip. Because once Time stops and we start running again, if you lose your hold, you'll be left behind.'

They each grabbed a shoulder, and I had to fight not to wince as their fingers dug in. I hit the button on the pen, and the roar of burning booths and stalls snapped off, replaced by the silence of the frozen world. I peered through the sullen red haze, and there was Mark, still striding straight toward us. The stopped Time hadn't slowed him one bit, and he was smiling now, in a cold anticipatory way. I hit the button again, and Time resumed. Sally and Melody let go of my shoulders and pushed me away, not even trying to hide their disappointment as I put my pen away.

'How is that even possible?' Melody said loudly.

'He's Mark Stone,' I said. 'Wherever he goes, he carries Hell with him. And what is done in Hell's sight has Hell's strength.'

'Do you think it would help if I said I was sorry?' said Sally.

Melody looked at her. 'What do you think?'

'There must be something we can do!' said Sally.

'I have an idea,' I said.

'Thank God,' said Sally.

'Exactly,' I said.

I moved over to a booth I'd just spotted, selling all kinds of religious symbols, because there are no atheist thieves when a job goes sour. I grabbed a handful of assorted crucifixes, and when I turned back, Mark was so close I could hear the crackling of his burning eyes. I threw the crosses on to the ground, so they formed a barrier between him and us. Mark stopped, contemplated the crucifixes for a moment, and then kicked them out of his way. He looked up, and I uncorked a vial of holy water and dashed the contents in his face, putting out his eyes.

Mark cried out and stumbled backwards, shaking his head. Melody and Sally and I were already off and running.

'Will that stop him?' Sally said hopefully.

'Not a hope in Hell,' I said. 'But it might slow him down. Have you still got your travel card?'

Sally searched quickly through her pockets and came up with the Ace of Thorns.

Melody glared at her. 'Why didn't you think of that before?'

'Because it was only programmed for the one journey: to bring us here!'

'Maybe I can open it from this side,' I said.

Sally inspected her card closely and then held it up to one ear. She stopped suddenly, and we stopped with her. Sally gave the card a good shake and listened again, and then looked at me.

'It's stopped buzzing,' she said. 'I think the batteries are dead.'

'OK . . .' I said. 'Plan two. I have a portable door I lifted from one of the stalls earlier.'

'You did *what*?' said Sally. 'If the scarecrows had spotted you stealing from the Bazaar, they would have ripped out all our insides, replaced them with stuffing and hung us on crosses! That's where new scarecrows come from!'

'I am Gideon Sable, and nowhere is off limits to me. That's the whole point of being a legendary master thief.'

'You used the time pen, didn't you?' said Melody.

'Oh, please,' I said. 'The quickness of the hand deceives the eye.'

'That actually worked in a place like this?' said Sally.

'You didn't see anything,' I said calmly. 'And you were standing right next to me when I did it.'

'Why haven't we used the door before this?' Melody said loudly.

'Because I had hoped to get far enough away that Mark wouldn't know we had it,' I said. 'Making it harder for him to follow us. But needs must when the hellhound's on your trail.'

I produced the portable door from inside my jacket pocket, and the thick black blob pulsed in my hand, eager to be put to work. I slapped it against the nearest booth wall, and the blob stretched out to form a perfectly ordinary-looking door. I turned the brass handle, opened the door and hurried through, with Melody and Sally treading on my heels. And we stepped out of a wall in Soho.

I peeled the door off the wall, and it shrank quickly back into a blob. I tucked it in my pocket and then listened carefully to the wall, but there was no sound of Mark coming after us. I let my breath out in a slow sigh and relaxed a little. Melody and Sally leaned on me as they got their breath back.

'Can he still come after us?' Sally said finally.

'Of course,' I said. 'But Hogge's club has security protections only one step down from the Whispering Gallery, so we should disappear off Mark's radar. By the time he's tracked us here, we'll have rescued our friends and be well on our way to Box Tunnel Hill. And I don't think even a hellhound could follow us into the Preserve.'

'Can I have that in writing?' said Melody.

'If you want,' I said.

It was still the early hours of the morning, in the darkest part of Soho, where neon blazed like a working girl's come-on, and every sin you could think of was beckoning from a street corner. Sally stabbed a finger at the club on the other side of the street.

'That's it! That's Hogge's place!'

'I know,' I said patiently. 'That's why I had the door bring us here.'

Sally glowered at me. 'Have you been to this club before?'

'A long time ago,' I said. 'When I was somebody else. I had hoped I'd never have to come here again.'

I put Mark Stone out of my mind, so I could concentrate on Hogge. I looked quickly up and down the street. The few people still searching for some trouble to get into were going out of their way to not even glance at Hogge's club, even when they had to dart right past it. The sign over the door said, *Hogge Heaven*. The façade was ugly and functional, with none of the usual hot neon, because the kind of people who came to Hogge Heaven already knew what it had to offer and didn't need to be tempted in. You would have needed a fair-sized gun to keep most of them out.

'There's no muscle out front,' Sally said quietly. 'Could Hogge have taken his prisoners somewhere else?'

'No,' I said. 'Hogge doesn't run.'

'Then why isn't there anyone guarding the door?' said Melody.

I had to smile. 'This is a trap, remember? Hogge wants us to go in. And just because you can't see any security, it doesn't mean there isn't any.'

Melody scowled. 'I feel the need for weapons. Something seriously big and shooty, to help even the odds.'

I looked at her. 'We don't do weapons.'

'Speak for yourself, darling,' said Sally.

'The Damned usually takes care of the rough stuff,' said Melody. 'Or Polly, in her wolf mode. But we're on our own now. You can bet Hogge's people will have weapons.'

'And they'll have a lot more practice when it comes to using them,' I said. 'If we play the game by Hogge's rules, we'll lose. Because he's been doing it a lot longer than we have. We need to out-think him.'

Melody nodded reluctantly. 'So, what's the plan? In through the front door or sneak round the back? Doesn't really matter; just show me a door, and I'll kick it in and walk right over whatever's on the other side.'

'No, you won't,' I said firmly. 'Hogge has protections like you wouldn't believe. Starting with doors that kick back.'

'I still have my membership card,' said Sally.

'No need,' I said. 'Hogge wants us to come to him. But you have to expect him to indulge in a little fun along the way.'

'Really not liking the sound of that,' said Melody.

'Our advantage is that he doesn't know me,' I said. 'Only the man I used to be, before I became Gideon Sable.'

'Why does he want you so badly?' Melody said bluntly.

'Because I spat in his piggy eye and got away with it,' I said. 'Hogge knew Lex and Polly were part of my crew. The whole point of this meeting is to rub my nose in what he's done to them and see how much he can make me pay to get my people back. But even though Hogge lives for a chance to get even, he never lets it get in the way of making a profit. That's what I'm counting on.'

'So you do have a plan,' said Sally.

'Always,' I said. 'Now, let's go see what the big man has waiting for us.'

'After you,' said Sally.

'Damn right,' said Melody.

I crossed the street with both of them hanging well back, ready to use me as a human shield if necessary. I stopped a cautious distance away from the main door, looked it over carefully and then pushed it open, bracing myself for everything from a lightning bolt to a bucket of whitewash. Hogge's sense of humour tended towards the crude. But nothing happened, so I pressed on into a deserted underlit lobby completely lacking in frills or comforts. A dim shape was standing on the other side of the room. I moved cautiously forward until I was standing before a shrunken figure in a shabby suit, with a gaunt face and haunted eyes. An iron collar had been locked around his throat, and a heavy chain attached him to the nearest wall.

'Maurice?' I said. 'What the hell are you doing here?'

'You know this guy?' said Melody.

'I used to, back in the day,' I said. 'I thought you had enough sense to stay away from places like this, Maurice.'

His mouth twitched in something like a smile. 'Good sense was never my long suit. You're looking good . . .?'

'Gideon, these days,' I said. 'You look like shit, Maurice.'

'How did you know this guy?' said Melody.

'He used to be a whale,' I said. 'A big-time gambler, indulged by Hogge because he always bet big and usually lost. What are you doing here, Maurice?'

'You'd be amazed how far a man can fall when he puts his mind to it,' said Maurice. 'Even my family fortune turned out to have a limit, much to my surprise. And when I had nothing left, Hogge put me to work here, paying off my debt one day at a time.'

'Doing what?' said Sally, fascinated in spite of herself.

'Whatever Hogge tells me to do,' said Maurice.

'How long do you have to do this?' I said.

'Given the interest on my debt, forever and a day,' said Maurice. And he showed me his twitch of a smile again.

'I'll talk to Hogge,' I said. 'Find some way to make your freedom part of my deal.'

'Why would you do that?' said Maurice. 'It's not like we were ever close.'

'Because some things are just wrong,' I said.

Maurice nodded slowly and then leaned forward as much as his chain would allow.

'Hogge has plans for you, Gideon. Get out of here, while you still can.'

'Hogge has no idea what I have planned for him,' I said.

Maurice managed something like a real smile. 'If you get the chance, push his face into the trough and hold it there until he drowns.'

'That is the plan,' I said.

The chain suddenly ratcheted off into the wall, jerking Maurice away from me. He stumbled and almost fell, but I moved quickly forward to hold him up. Maurice shook his head and pushed me away.

'The more you try to help, the more he'll hurt me to get at you. Go on, Gideon. You don't want to keep Hogge waiting.'

He waved at the door behind him, and it opened on its own. I didn't look back as I led Melody and Sally through, because I knew Maurice would have turned his face away. He might have fallen, but he still remembered the man he used to be.

'Take your cue from me,' I murmured to Sally and Melody. 'And don't start any trouble until we've seen the lay of the land.'

'And then?' said Melody.

'First, I shall reason with the man,' I said.

'And if that doesn't work?' said Sally.

'Then let it all kick off, big time,' I said.

'Now you're talking my language,' said Melody.

'Hogge has someone on his payroll strong enough to take down the Damned,' Sally said sharply.

'I hadn't forgotten,' I said.

The main level of Hogge Heaven turned out to be completely empty. Great splashes of blood decorated the walls and floor – more than I would have expected from even the most extreme fun and games.

'Where is everybody?' said Melody.

'In the wind,' I said. 'Hogge wants us all to himself.'

'But he enjoyed showing off his captives to the people downstairs,' said Sally.

'It'll be deserted down there now,' I said. 'Hogge knows he'll have to make some kind of deal with me, and he won't want any witnesses.'

A man came striding out of the shadows, his footsteps hammering on the floor, until he could stand right before us and ostentatiously block our way.

'Digby,' I said. 'I should have known you'd still be here, sniffing around Hogge's arse.'

'Where else should I be?' said Digby in a flat colourless voice. 'My place is with my master, who supplies me with pleasures and opportunities far beyond your limited imagination.'

It had been some time since we'd last met, but Digby hadn't changed. Still big and brutal in his butler's formal outfit, untouched and unmoved by whatever happened around him.

Melody sniffed loudly. 'Gideon, who is this person?'

The open contempt in her voice warmed my heart. 'This is Hogge's right-hand man,' I said. 'For when he wants something scratched. Functionary, bodyguard and thug to the trade. An unstoppable force in an ill-fitting suit.'

Digby looked down his nose at me. 'I was told you were a whole new person these days, but you're the same unfunny little man you always were.'

I nodded to Melody and Sally. 'Don't let the servant's look fool you. Some time ago, Digby persuaded someone he still won't talk about to cut him out of the world with a psychic scalpel. Now, nothing in this world can change or affect him, because he's no longer a part of it. Of course, he has no connection to anyone, either. No one gives a damn about him, because he's not really here.'

'You don't miss what you never had,' said Digby.

I felt a moment of sympathy until I remembered some of the things I'd seen Digby do. Melody and Sally were studying him carefully; they knew a predator when they saw one. Digby ignored them, his gaze fixed on me.

'Hogge is waiting,' he said flatly. 'Your little friends can stay here.'

'I don't go anywhere without my crew,' I said immediately. 'Either you agree to that, or we turn around and walk right out of here. And you can explain to Hogge how you let us go.'

'You would abandon the people we've already taken from you?' said Digby.

'If need be,' I said.

Give Hogge even the slightest advantage, and he'd walk all over me. If I was to have any chance in the negotiations, he had to believe I was prepared to be as unreasonable as him. Digby shrugged.

'Very well, you can bring your pets with you. But keep them under control, or I'll put them on a leash.'

I nodded to Sally and Melody. 'Stick close, and don't get provoked into starting anything we can't finish.'

'Please,' said Sally. 'We are professionals.'

'Damn right,' said Melody.

Digby led the way through the door at the back and down the stairs, while I and my crew followed at a cautious distance. Halfway down, I paused, my attention caught by the sound of thunder approaching at speed and then fading away.

'What was that?' said Melody.

'An Underground train,' I said. 'There must be a tunnel somewhere close.'

'How very interesting,' said Melody. 'Now, can we please get a move on? I am really looking forward to meeting your old friend Hogge.'

'This isn't about him,' Sally said sharply. 'It's about rescuing Lex and Polly.'

'One step at a time,' I said.

We finally emerged on to the deserted lower level of the club, and the first thing I saw was Lex and Polly in their cages. Sally made a low sound of distress and started to push past me. I stopped her with an out-thrust arm.

'Don't give Hogge the satisfaction.'

'I will have his heart's blood for this,' said Sally.

'Of course you will,' I said. 'But later.'

Polly Perkins was sitting naked in her cage, her coffee-coloured skin sleek with sweat, her long dark hair hanging down around her lowered face. She slowly turned to look at us, and then fought the silver chain so she could press her face against the bars of the cage. The silver collar burned her as it dug into her throat, but Polly didn't flinch.

'Get out,' she said, her voice an exhausted whisper. 'It's a trap.'

'We know,' I said. 'Don't worry. I have a plan.'

She managed a small smile and sat back again. 'It had better be a really good one, Gideon. Because I'm all out of ideas.'

'All my plans are good,' I said.

Her smile widened for a moment. 'That has not always been my experience.'

Lex Talon, the Damned, sat slumped in his cage. I'd thought Sally's description had prepared me, but the mess someone had made of Lex's face made me want to turn mine away. The empty eye sockets were caked with dried blood. Sally was pressing hard against my arm, and I could hear Melody breathing harshly behind me.

'He's alive,' I said. 'That means there's hope.'

'How is he still alive?' said Melody.

'The halos at his wrists are glowing,' I said.

'Do you think there's a chance they might heal him, once we get him out of here?' said Sally.

'I don't know,' I said. 'But I can't help feeling that if the halos could have done more, they would have by now. Hold it together, Sally. Once my business with Hogge is done, we'll

take Lex and Polly with us. And then we can think about
revenge.'

I gestured for Sally and Melody to stay put and walked
forward to stand before Hogge. He looked just as I remembered. A great beast of a man, who had feasted on everything
the world had to offer and still wanted more. A massive
sprawling figure, he wore a shapeless Hawaiian shirt over
tightly stretched shorts and sat at his ease on the throne he'd
had specially made for him. Solid steel to support his weight,
with piled-up cushions for comfort. Hogge looked as though
it would take a crane to get him on and off his throne, but I
had no doubt there was still muscle under the fat. He had a
square, shaven head, a flat face with deep-set eyes and a pursed
mouth that only smiled at the prospect of someone hurting.

'Looking good, Hogge,' I said easily. 'You lose a few
pounds?'

He smiled at me. 'Gideon Sable . . . Such a pleasure to see
you again.'

His voice was calm and cultured, thoughtful and precise. A
man who knew the value of hate and fear, and how to make
them work for him. Digby took up a position at his master's
left hand, waiting to be told what to do. I ignored him, so I
could give my full attention to the man standing at Hogge's
right hand. An elegant Chinese gentleman, in an immaculate
cream-coloured suit. He bowed politely to me, and I nodded
to him. Hogge gestured at his new man with a large meaty
hand.

'This is how I was able to humble the mighty Damned.
Allow me to present Mr Chang, master of weaponized fate.'

Chang winced, just a little, as though unhappy with the
casual summary of a far more complicated concept. He shot
me a *What can you do?* look, and when he spoke, his voice
was an aristocratic drawl.

'Destiny runs through the world like an unseen river, rushing
ever on, changing everything it touches. My studies have
taught me just where to dip my hand into these turbulent
waters and alter the flow to change the world. I can make
things happen and not happen, or happen differently, as I
choose.'

'Then why aren't you master of the world?' I said. 'Instead of serving a cheap thug like Hogge?'

Chang shrugged eloquently. 'The process is not easy. It takes a lot out of me. And I have to be very careful, because every time I change the world, I run the risk of changing myself. The process is complicated, and I need to understand it better. Since this learning promises to be long and expensive, I must go where the work is. I serve Hogge for the money. For now.'

'You serve me until I tell you otherwise,' said Hogge, not looking at Chang. His deep-set eyes were fixed entirely on me. 'Would you like to see how I brought your friends down, my dear Gideon? I promise you'll find it most instructive.'

He gestured heavily and a vision appeared, hanging in the air like a mirage. It showed Hogge watching happily as a naked Polly Perkins was dragged before him. The young Indian woman fought fiercely to break away but couldn't even loosen the grip Digby had on her arm. The watching crowd laughed and pointed and jeered at her, until Hogge gestured for them to be silent. They all stood still, watching hungrily, anticipating the suffering and humiliations to come.

'You dance divinely, my dear,' said Hogge. 'But you are also a spy and must suffer the consequences.'

'And you're the bad guy,' said Polly. 'Which means you'll get what's coming to you.'

'With a little help from your friends, perhaps?' said Hogge. 'Gideon Sable's illustrious crew? You think they'll come charging to your rescue? My dear, I'm counting on it.'

'I don't need their help,' said Polly.

A tide of dark fur swept over her from head to toe, as the dancer gave way to the wolf. The huge beast howled triumphantly and sent Digby flying through the air with one sweep of her muscular arm. She crouched, to launch herself at Hogge's throat, and then Chang took a step forward and smiled at her, and the wolf was a dancer once more. Polly stumbled and almost fell, shocked at having her feral self ripped away. She tried to change back again and couldn't, and while she was distracted, Digby snapped a silver collar around her throat. Polly howled miserably as the silver burned her, and she dropped to her knees. Digby fastened a length of silver chain to the collar and then wrapped it quickly around Polly's body in loops that burned her flesh wherever they touched. She shook and shuddered, crying out in pain.

Digby dragged her over to the waiting cage. Polly fought him every inch of the way but couldn't even slow Digby down. He opened the door, threw her in, connected the chain to the bars and locked the door.

Hogge laughed softly. His eyes burned as he studied Polly's writhing form, savouring her hate and her helplessness.

The vision changed, to show Lex Talon striding through the lower level. The crowd fell back, scattering quickly to get out of his way. A huge and overbearing presence, with broad shoulders and a barrel chest, the Damned wore only faded jeans and the shining bracelets at his wrists. His hairy torso gleamed with sweat, but his eyes were cold and his mouth was a thin flat line. His face looked as though it had been carved out of stone. He stopped right in front of Hogge.

'Release Polly,' he said. 'And I'll let you live.'

Hogge smiled. 'I knew you'd find your way here eventually, my dear Lex. To get what's yours. The question is, what are you prepared to pay for it?'

'No one threatens my family,' said Lex.

'But she's my little pet now,' said Hogge.

The halos at Lex's wrists glowed fiercely and his armour swept over him, sealing him off from the world. Angelic armour, from Above and Below. It didn't so much cover Lex as replace him, a greater thing overwriting a lesser. The whole crowd retreated, crying out in shock and horror as something terrible was born into the world. The darkness on the Damned's left side wasn't just the absence of light but a hole in the world, and the light on his right side blazed like a piece of the sun come down to Earth. Heaven and Hell made manifest in the world.

Hogge shrank back on his throne and gestured desperately to Chang, who frowned hard, concentrating on the Damned. For a long moment, nothing happened. A single bead of sweat ran down Chang's face. And the Damned's armour disappeared. Lex looked at the bracelets on his wrists, but they weren't even glowing. And then Digby moved in behind Lex and struck him a terrible blow to the head.

Lex dropped to one knee, and Digby hit him in the face again and again, grunting with the effort he put into his blows, giving Lex no chance to recover. Lex fell to the floor, his features a bloody mess, only half conscious. And that was when Digby took out a knife and went to work on Lex's eyes.

The vision snapped off. Hogge applauded, slamming his great hands together. I looked at Chang.

'You made that possible. You should start running, because I've seen the Damned come back from far worse than this.'

'It all comes down to fate,' Chang said calmly. 'Those who control it, and those who suffer from it. Given how much violence and suffering the Damned has inflicted on this world, I do not feel he has any right to object when it is turned upon him.'

'He was trying to be a better man,' I said.

Chang shrugged. 'Aren't we all?'

'Run,' I said. 'Lex has friends.'

'A threat?' said Chang. 'From a miserable thief and his two little helpers? Destiny is not so easily averted.'

'Destiny is bullshit,' said Melody.

She stepped forward to stand beside me, seething with barely repressed fury. Sally moved in on my other side, and I'd never seen her look so cold and focused. Hogge smiled easily at all of us.

'Mr Digby, I think our friends could profit from a demonstration of just what we're prepared to do. Bring our good and faithful servant down here.'

Digby gathered up a length of chain lying beside Hogge's throne and pulled on it. After a moment, there was the sound of footsteps descending the stairs. I turned to face them, and Melody and Sally pressed in close beside me. We tensed, ready to take on whatever reinforcements Hogge had summoned, but it was only Maurice, hauled along by the chain attached to his collar. Digby kept up a steady pressure until Maurice finally came to a halt before Hogge. He swayed on his feet, his eyes lowered submissively.

Hogge smiled at him. 'My dear Maurice, I am happy to

inform you that your term of servitude is at an end. All you have to do is provide me one last service, and your debt is paid in full.'

Maurice finally raised his head to look at Hogge, almost afraid to hope.

'What do I have to do?'

'Die,' said Hogge.

Digby grabbed Maurice's head with both hands and ripped it off his shoulders. For a moment, the headless body just stood there, blood fountaining from the ragged neck, and then the knees gave way and the body fell to the floor. Digby held the severed head before him, so he could smile into the fading eyes, and then he dropped it on the floor and stamped on it. The skull collapsed like a paper bag.

By the time I had the time pen in my hand, it was all over. I took a step toward Digby, and he swung around to face me. His smile defied me to do anything about all the awful things he'd done. So I smiled back at him, letting my grin spread wide as I held his gaze with mine. Digby saw the cold certainty in my eyes, and for the first time he stirred uneasily. He looked to Hogge for orders. And that was when I knew I had him.

I hit the button on my pen and Time slammed to a halt. A heavy crimson glow filled the lower level, and in the sudden silence everyone else became a statue. Including Digby. I allowed myself a quiet moment of relief. I'd gambled that while Digby was unstoppable in the world, he was still vulnerable to the passing of Time. I might not be able to kill him, but there were still ways to punish him.

I forced my way through the sullen inertia of paused Time, took off Digby's jacket and replaced it back to front. I made a point of moving to a different position before I restarted Time and put the pen away, so everyone would know something had happened. They all jumped a little, and then Sally laughed and pointed at Digby. Everyone turned to look as he stared down at his reversed jacket. Hogge looked at me sharply.

'So, dear boy, the rumours are true. You have a time device. How typical of you, to choose such an annoying toy. But I'm sure I shall enjoy playing with it. Mister Digby . . .'

'Hold it!' I said. 'I just stopped Time so I could slip another of my little toys into Digby's pocket. It's called a Time Accelerator, and it does what it says on the lid. All I have to do is hit the remote, and Time will speed up until there's nothing left of him but dust. So behave yourself, Digby, or Hogge will have to send someone out for a dustpan and brush.'

Digby's hands started toward his pockets and then stopped. He looked at Hogge, who looked at me.

'Why didn't you place this nasty little device on my person?'

'Because I'm very annoyed with Digby,' I said. 'But don't worry, Hogge, I'll get around to you. In time.'

Hogge nodded slowly. 'My little boy is all grown up. You've acquired a backbone since your time with me.'

'I could kill you with a thought,' I said. 'Or Sally could swap out important parts of your body for whatever similar-sized objects happen to be lying around. And you have no idea what my illustrious colleague Melody Mead is capable of. You should never have let us get this close, Hogge. You should never have let this get personal.'

He smiled. 'Where you and I are concerned, it's always going to be personal. Mr Chang, is there nothing you can do?'

Chang was already shaking his head. 'Their ways are hidden from me. Their gifts are not of this world and make it impossible to see what they have in mind.'

'We shall have words about this later, Mr Chang,' said Hogge. He turned his gaze back to me. 'It seems you have the advantage, dear boy. But while Mr Digby is valuable to me, I have a whole organization of talented people at my command. Do you really think you can rescue your friends by threatening one man?'

'No,' I said. 'That's not why I'm here. I want to buy them back.'

Hogge laughed softly. 'Now this is more like it! Very well. I am ready to consider any reasonable offer. But you must understand that I expect to make a considerable profit by auctioning off the Damned and the werewolf. Do you really have the resources to outbid so many interested parties?'

'I'm not talking about money or the services of me and my crew,' I said steadily. 'I'm offering to buy Lex and Polly back with information. Which is only good in the short term. If you want to make the deal, you're going to have to agree now.' I showed him my most confident smile. 'Trust me; it'll be worth it.'

'Agreed, my dear young friend,' said Hogge. 'In return for this profitable information, I will release the Damned and the wolf into your care.'

So I told him about the Preserve. What it was, where it was and all the wonders it contained. Once they realized what I was doing, Melody and Sally raised their voices in protest, but I just talked over them. I could see the hunger growing in Hogge's eyes as I described the treasure house of the Preserve, but while I told him all about the Box Tunnel complex, I carefully didn't mention the secret side tunnel. Or my dealings with Sharpe and Jacobi. Or the ghost.

'If you want to act on this information, you need to start now,' I said. 'Partly because my crew and I will also be going after the Preserve, but mostly because the government is talking about blowing it all up with the nuke under the floorboards. And you know what twitchy trigger fingers those people have.'

'Very well,' said Hogge. 'A treasure house in the hand trumps a potential profit. You have your deal, Mr Sable.'

'No!' said Digby. 'We can't let the Damned go! Not after everything we went through to put him in that cage!'

'I have agreed to the deal,' Hogge said reproachfully.

'But the Damned will come after me!' said Digby. 'Because of what I did, on your orders!'

Hogge raised an eyebrow. 'Mr Digby . . . I do hope you're not blaming me for your present predicament.'

Digby spun around to glare at me. 'You're bluffing about the Time Accelerator . . . Because if it was real, you would have used it. So I'm going to play with your little girlfriend until she breaks. Stop me if you can.'

I looked at Hogge, but he just smiled and watched to see what I would do. My hand went to the time pen again, but Digby was already throwing himself at Melody, his hands straining for her throat. Melody grabbed his nearest outstretched arm, pirouetted neatly and tossed Digby over her shoulder. He hit the ground hard, and Melody twisted his arm against the joint until he howled, to hold him in place. She smiled around her.

'Size isn't everything.'

She turned Digby over on to his back and stabbed two stiffened fingers into his eyes. He cried out miserably, and then the sound cut off abruptly as she kicked him in the groin with such force she lifted his body off the floor. Digby curled up around his pain, breath whistling in his throat.

'Ouch,' I said.

'Just because he can't be destroyed,' said Melody, 'doesn't mean he can't be hurt.'

'Let me hurt him,' said Sally. 'I'll bet I can make him scream the house down if I swap out his heart for a piece of junk.'

'No,' I said. 'Let's give him to Polly.' I turned to Hogge. 'Unlock the cages.'

'Mr Digby is very valuable to me,' said Hogge.

'How valuable is your word?' I said. 'We made a deal.'

'So we did,' said Hogge. He nodded at the cages. 'Unlock.'

Both cage doors swung open, and so did the silver collar around Polly's throat. She shook her head quickly and the collar fell away, taking the chain with it. Digby was just struggling up on to his feet when Polly stepped out of her cage. She stood up straight and stretched slowly. Over six feet tall, lean and muscular, her eyes blazed fiercely as she fixed her gaze on Digby. He sneered back at her, and she growled at him. A deep, disturbing sound.

Black fur swept slowly over her, taking its time. Her back arched, her muscles bulged, and bones cracked loudly as her arms and legs lengthened. Polly Perkins became a huge humanoid wolf. Her face jutted forward, forming a long muzzle packed with teeth. Vicious claws protruded from her hair-covered hands. Her eyes glowed golden. And when she growled again, I could feel the sound reverberate in my bones.

Digby stood his ground and laughed in the wolf's face. 'Bad dog . . .'

Polly surged forward inhumanly quickly, hitting Digby in

the chest with such force she bowled him right off his feet. He crashed to the floor with a giant wolf sitting on his chest. A clawed hand ripped his face right off the skull, and his screams were choked by a sudden rush of blood. Polly took Digby to pieces with her teeth and claws, every blow driven by the helpless rage she'd felt as she watched Digby mutilate Lex. She couldn't kill Digby, but she could still make a real mess of him. And she did.

As a final touch, she bit the eyes out of his head.

Polly finally stepped back from the bloody wreckage shuddering and moaning on the floor and turned to face Hogge.

'No, Polly,' I said quickly. 'Later. We have a deal.'

Polly turned her back on Hogge and stalked over to Lex's cage, where Melody and Sally were struggling to manhandle the unconscious body through the door. I couldn't help them. I had to keep my eye on Hogge and Chang. Polly pulled Lex out of the cage with one hand and slung him over her shoulder in a fireman's lift. He didn't make a sound.

'Let's get the hell out of here,' said Polly.

'Sounds like a plan to me,' I said.

'Digby will recover,' said Hogge. 'He always does. And Chang will work out some way to compensate for your crew's annoying but limited talents. And then . . .'

'You come after any of my crew,' I said, 'and I'll be back.'

'Of course you will,' said Hogge. 'That was always the point. To have you here, with me. Where you belong.'

I turned my back on him and headed for the stairs, followed by Sally and Melody, and the wolf Polly carrying Lex.

'I can't believe we're just leaving,' Sally said grimly. 'Without making Hogge pay for everything he did!'

'Later,' I said.

'You keep saying that,' said Melody.

'Because I mean it,' I said.

'I can't believe you got away with that Time Accelerator bluff again,' Melody said quietly.

'What makes you think I was bluffing?' I said.

And that was when Hogge raised his voice again. 'Just one moment, if you please . . .'

I looked back to see Hogge smiling easily from his throne,

with Digby standing on one side, completely restored, and Chang on the other.

'You didn't really think you could just walk away, did you?' said Hogge. 'Not when we have so much unfinished business between us?'

'We have nothing more to say to each other,' I said. 'We made a deal.'

'I only promised to release Lex and Polly from their cages,' said Hogge. 'And now you've given me all the details about the Preserve . . .'

I had to smile. 'You think I gave you all the details?'

Hogge shrugged heavily. 'I know what I need to know. Ah, Gideon, my dear old friend . . . You wouldn't believe the number of people I have waiting to bid on your crew, for all kinds of reasons. Come back, Gideon. And sit at my feet again.'

'Not going to happen,' I said.

Hogge raised an eyebrow. 'You think you have a choice? You should have remembered, dear boy: no one betrays me and gets away with it.'

I smiled and gestured at the stairs. 'Listen to that rumble, Hogge. That is the sound of an Underground train roaring through its tunnel. Allow us to leave, or I will divert that train and bring it crashing through the wall. Aimed right at you.'

Hogge thought for a moment and then laughed softly. 'You have come a long way, Gideon. Well played, dear boy. Off you go. We'll meet again.'

'I'm planning on it,' I said.

We set off up the stairs. Melody moved in close beside me and lowered her voice.

'Were you bluffing about the train, Gideon?'

I smiled. 'What do you think?'

FIVE

Council of War

The street outside the club was perfectly empty. No traffic, no pedestrians, nothing moving anywhere in the long sullen silence of the night. I stopped my crew outside the door and looked carefully up and down the deserted street.

'Does anyone else feel like they have a bullseye painted on them?' said Melody.

Polly looked quickly around, her fur bristling. 'You think Hogge had the street cleared so his people could do something nasty to us without any witnesses?'

'That does sound like him,' I said.

'But there's no one here!' said Melody.

'She's not wrong,' said Polly. 'I can smell a whole bunch of things on the night air, including a few that are scouring out the insides of my nostrils, but there's not a trace of people anywhere. There are craters on the Moon that have more nightlife than this.'

'We can't stay here, Gideon,' Sally said urgently. 'Lex needs help.'

'I think I might know where we can find him some,' I said.

I set off down the empty street at a good pace, and Melody immediately moved in beside me. The others stuck close behind. Our footsteps echoed loudly in the quiet, as though trying to attract someone's attention. The shadows remained still and unoccupied, and no one emerged from a side street with bad intent. It was as though we had the whole night to ourselves. But even with the overwhelming sense of unease, it wasn't long before Melody started up again.

'You didn't have to tell Hogge everything about the Box Tunnel heist,' she said sharply. 'Why make it easy for him?'

'I didn't,' I said. 'I only gave Hogge the what and the where

– enough to tempt him and keep his thoughts occupied. We're still in the best position to get to the Preserve first.'

'Even if we do get there before Hogge,' said Melody, 'you honestly think you can steal a ghost?'

I glanced back at Sally and Polly. They were clearly listening but choosing not to get involved. I kept my voice carefully calm and assured.

'I've stolen far more difficult things than ghosts. And while Hogge might be the head of a criminal organization, he doesn't do the hands-on thing. He'll have to put a crew together to do the job for him, and that will take time.'

'He already has Digby and Chang,' said Melody, not giving an inch.

'They'd be out of their depth the moment they entered the complex,' I said patiently. 'Hogge is going to need specialized operatives – like us – and they're never easy to come by at short notice. We can get in, do the job and get out again long before Hogge's people turn up. Now, may I suggest we concentrate on putting this whole area behind us? Hogge has never prided himself on being a good loser.'

Polly cleared her throat, an odd sound from a large and hairy werewolf. 'Can I just remind everyone that I have an unconscious body slumped over my shoulder that isn't getting any lighter?'

'But you're a werewolf!' said Melody.

'Not for much longer,' said Polly. 'We're bound to start bumping into people soon.'

'Why are all of you being so casual?' said Sally. 'Lex is hurt!'

'He's the Damned,' said Polly. 'He's tough. Have faith in the man.'

'Anyone will break if you hit them hard enough,' said Sally. 'And I've never seen Lex hurt this badly.'

'He'll hold on till we can get him some help,' I said confidently. 'Lex is built to take punishment, as well as hand it out.'

'He's burning up!' said Sally. 'And I don't like the way he's breathing. We have to get him to a hospital!'

'Regular hospitals ask too many questions,' I said. 'I know

a few off-the-books operations, with twilight doctors and night nurses who only ever ask one question: *Are you sure you can pay the bill?* But even there, you can bet someone would talk. And then all the Damned's enemies will come crashing through the woodwork, hot for the chance to pay off old grudges and glory in their revenge.'

Polly growled. 'Let them come. They'd have to get through me to get to him.'

'We'll all stand by him,' I said patiently. 'But even we might not be enough to protect Lex from some of the enemies he's made.'

'What about Sandra Ransom?' said Melody. 'She helped us before. Call her.'

For a long moment, none of us said anything. Sandra Ransom was not a name to raise lightly. I don't think anyone knows for sure exactly who or what she is, but given the scary levels of power she can call on, most people refer to her as God's little sister.

'I will call her if there's no other option,' I said. 'But she can be the perfect example of the cure that's worse than the problem.'

'We're wasting time!' said Sally. 'Lex looks like he's at death's door! Why aren't we doing anything?'

'We are,' I said. 'We're taking him to Madam Osiris.'

I didn't need to look around to know they were all looking at each other, and not in a good way.

'I don't think we need a fortune teller right now, do we?' said Melody.

'Madam Osiris has always been a lot more than that,' I said.

'That's true,' said Melody. 'She used to be a whole bunch of other people, some of whom tried to kill us!'

'But they're gone now,' I said. 'All that's left is a woman of hidden depths and surprising powers, including a remarkable ability for thinking around corners.'

'What makes you think she won't sell Lex out to his enemies the moment our backs are turned?' said Sally.

'Because she's still scared of the potential future she saw, where the Damned killed her,' I said. 'Having Lex be grateful to her for saving his life should go a long way to making sure that future never happens.'

Melody frowned. 'Last I heard, Madam Osiris was seriously off the grid and under the radar. Do you even know where to start looking for her?'

'I make it a point to know where everyone is,' I said. 'If only so I can be sure which direction they'll choose when they come for me. Madam Osiris is currently hiding out in Brighton. She always goes to ground there when she's feeling vulnerable, because she knows she can count on enough general supernatural skulduggery to make sure she won't stand out.'

I stopped abruptly, and everyone piled up around me. I studied the empty scene carefully, making sure we had the street to ourselves.

'I think we've put enough distance between us and the club that Hogge's security people won't be able to pick up on what we're doing. So let's get this show on the road.'

I slapped my portable door against a nearby wall, and the blob immediately spread out to form a perfectly ordinary door, complete with brass letterbox and handle. Because the blobs know all there is to know about camouflage. But when I tried the handle, it refused to turn. I shot a quick smile at the others, to show I wasn't in the least embarrassed.

'Madam Osiris always has a few protections in place. Because she needs them.'

I sank down on one knee, with as much dignity as I could muster, and shouted through the letterbox.

'Madam Osiris! This is Gideon Sable!'

There was a pause, and then a familiar voice answered me.

'Never heard of you . . . go away . . . no one of that name here!'

'You're not fooling anyone,' I said sternly. 'And since I am very definitely Gideon Sable, if I have to unlock this door the hard way, you'll never be able to close what's left of it again.'

The voice said, 'Oh, shit!' and then had nothing more to say. I stood up and nodded to the others.

'She just needed to be reminded who her friends are.'

'Yes,' said Melody. 'I thought you sounded very friendly.'

The door still hadn't opened, so I banged on it with my fist. 'Last chance, before I make a hole in your world so big you couldn't plug it with an elephant's arse!'

'Look,' said Madam Osiris's voice. 'It really isn't very convenient just at the moment. Couldn't you try again later?'

'No,' I said. 'On the grounds that it isn't at all convenient where we are.'

'Oh, all right! But you'll just have to take us as you find us.'

Melody raised an eyebrow and mouthed, *Us?* I shrugged. The door unlocked itself and we hurried through.

The door slammed shut the moment we were all inside and couldn't wait to turn itself back into a blob, as though embarrassed at finding itself in a small and shabby bed-sitting room. I peeled it off the faded wallpaper and tucked it away in my jacket pocket. As usual, Madam Osiris was keeping her lighting deliberately low, to maintain the proper atmosphere for peering into her crystal ball, divining the future and fleecing her clients. Heavy drapes covered the only window, and what illumination there was came from a dozen black candles scattered around the room. I had to smile. Madam Osiris's gifts were perfectly real, but she knew the punters would only accept her predictions if they came presented in the proper manner. In her game, you had to be fake to seem real.

A Baron Samedi skeleton smiled toothily from the far corner, wearing a smart black funeral suit with a top hat tilted rakishly over its bony brow. A spotted snake stirred lethargically in its ribcage. Several Hands of Glory stood in a row on a battered chest of drawers and greeted our appearance with a languid round of applause. Shelves of bottles, jars and other less orthodox containers covered all of one wall, containing mandrake root and John the Conqueror, vampire teeth that clattered angrily against the inside of the glass as they tried to gnaw their way out, and what looked like traditional boiled sweets.

Madam Osiris was standing beside a fold-down bed with rumpled bedclothes, wrapped in a shabby black dressing gown covered in all thirteen signs of the zodiac. A handsome woman of a certain age, she still looked as if she could fight her corner.

Her eyes had long ago been replaced by glowing crystal balls, which, if nothing else, showed commitment to her chosen path. She draped a possessive arm around the waist of the glowering young man standing next to her. A splendid physical specimen wearing nothing but gleaming white boxer shorts, he had floppy blonde hair, pale blue eyes and a sulky mouth.

'This is Jeremy,' said Madam Osiris, just a bit defiantly. 'He is my Sorceress's Apprentice. I'm teaching him everything I know.'

'I'm sure you are,' I said.

She sighed. 'Look, I needed someone to watch my back, all right?'

'And your front?' I said innocently.

'Well, obviously,' said Madam Osiris. 'Jeremy, this is the legendary master thief and complete pain in the arse, Gideon Sable, and his crew. I won't introduce them because they won't be staying long. Don't let them talk you into anything without checking with me first. Gideon, you and your people can speak freely in front of Jeremy, but don't get too close to him if you like having valuables.'

Jeremy smirked.

'Stop talking!' Sally said loudly. 'Lex needs help!'

'Keep a lid on it, dear,' said Madam Osiris. 'He's the Damned. The halos won't let him die. Not while they still have a use for him.'

She moved forward, and Polly turned around so Madam Osiris could get a good look at the man draped over her shoulder.

'Who the hell happened to him?' said Madam Osiris.

'Hogge,' I said. 'And Digby. And a new boy on the block, called Chang.'

Madam Osiris planted her hands on her bony hips, and the plastic bangles on her arms clattered loudly. She stuck her face in close to examine Lex's damaged features and then stepped back again.

'If you will play with the rough boys, you shouldn't be surprised when someone gets hurt. Chang . . . Can't say I know the name, but then I'm out of touch. Was a time I knew everyone in the scene, but now there are all these youngsters clawing their way up the ladder and trampling over anyone who doesn't get out of their way fast enough. I know, I know, concentrate on the Damned . . . No one cares about the small operator any more . . .'

She gestured sharply at the stuffed wendigos perched at the end of her bed, and they tumbled off on to the floor.

'Lay him down there and stand back. Let the dog see the rabbit.'

Sally looked at me.

'She knows what she's doing,' I said.

Polly laid Lex gently down on the bed, arranged him as comfortably as she could and then stepped away. Madam Osiris studied Lex thoughtfully, her crystal ball eyes glowing fiercely in the gloom.

'Can you fix him?' said Melody.

'Of course,' said Madam Osiris, not looking round. 'My eyes can see the present as clearly as the future. He might have taken one hell of a beating, but the halos are keeping him alive. In fact, give the man a few months' bed rest and quiet, and he'd be right as rain even without my help.'

'We don't have a few months,' I said.

'Obviously,' said Madam Osiris. 'Or you wouldn't be here, bothering me. All right, stand by for some dramatic rolling-up of the sleeves followed by industrial-strength hand gestures. What we need is a speeded-up restoration, with everything returned to factory settings.'

'But what about his eyes?' said Sally. Her voice broke on the last word.

'I could give him nice new crystal ones, like mine,' said Madam Osiris. 'But the halos would only reject them. They can be very jealous when it comes to protecting their property.'

Melody frowned. 'How do you know so much about the Damned and his halos?'

'Know your enemy,' said Madam Osiris. She frowned hard, weighing her options. 'There's a lot I could do, but you don't have the time, so . . . I think we'd better go with a shortcut.' She turned to Polly. 'Bite him.'

'*What?*' said Polly.

'Your bite will pass on the werewolf trait,' Madam Osiris

said patiently. 'Including your fast-healing ability. Just sink your teeth in and he'll be right as a trivet before you know it. The halos will purge the wolf trait from his system afterwards. They don't like to share.'

Polly looked to me, and I nodded. She leaned over the bed, glanced back at us somewhat self-consciously and then lowered her long wolf muzzle. Lex groaned briefly, as blood spilled on to the bedclothes. Polly carefully disengaged her jaws and stepped back from the bed, rubbing the back of a hairy hand across her grey lips. And then we all jumped as Lex suddenly sat up and stared around him with fully restored eyes.

'I feel great! What just happened?'

Sally let out a shriek of delight and dropped down beside Lex so she could hug him fiercely. Polly sat down on his other side, dropped a hairy arm across his shoulders and leaned her head against his. I exchanged a relieved glance with Melody and then inclined my head to Madam Osiris.

'I knew you could do it. Never doubted you for a moment.'

'Then why are you looking so relieved?' said Madam Osiris. 'I suppose there's no point mentioning my usual charges . . . No, I didn't think so. Just make sure the big man understands he owes me.' She nodded to Melody. 'Good to see you again, Annie.'

'I am not Annie! I am Melody Mead!'

'Of course you are, dear,' said Madam Osiris.

She studied Melody carefully with her glowing eyes and then moved over to stand beside me.

'Annie doesn't seem entirely herself at the moment,' she said quietly.

'She isn't,' I said, just as quietly. 'She's entirely taken up with being Melody.'

Madam Osiris smiled briefly. 'I know all there is to know about the problems of being different people. I'm still having trouble adjusting to being just me. Though Jeremy does help.'

'I'm sure he does,' I said.

We both looked at him, and he stirred uneasily.

'She's teaching me all kinds of things,' he said defiantly.

'I'm sure she is,' I said.

Sally was still hugging Lex tightly, as though afraid someone might take him away, while Polly kept patting Lex on the shoulder, as though to reassure herself he was still fine. Lex glowered at Madam Osiris and then fixed his gaze on me.

'Tell me there is a really good reason why I have ended up in the clutches of that woman.'

'You wish,' said Madam Osiris, and Jeremy smirked.

I brought Lex up to speed on what happened, and when I was done, he nodded to me and I nodded back. Because there are some things men just don't say to each other while they're sober. Madam Osiris cleared her throat loudly and then did it again until we both stared at her.

'You owe me your life, Lex Talon,' she said loudly.

Lex rubbed absently at his shoulder where Polly had bitten him and nodded brusquely to Madam Osiris.

'I'll remember.'

She smiled brightly and entirely artificially, then turned to me. 'Well, nice to see all of you again, but I'm sure you're in a hurry to be on your way . . .'

'One more thing,' I said.

The smile vanished. 'I should have known,' Madam Osiris said bitterly. 'What more do you need?'

'An unexpected way into the Box Tunnel complex,' I said.

She looked at me sharply. 'You're going after the Preserve? What do you want with that infamous repository for all that's bad and rotten in British Science? No, don't tell me; I don't want to know. Except I sort of do, because there's supposed to be some extremely valuable items locked away in that hellhole.' She paused and then frowned, as though looking at something only she could see. 'I could warn you about what's going to happen, but I already know you won't pay any attention, so what would be the point?'

'You can really see the future with those eyes?' said Polly.

'I get glimpses,' said Madam Osiris. 'But rarely enough to be useful. Which is why I have to lay it on with a trowel for the paying customers. They don't want the truth anyway – just something to keep them going, in the face of the inevitable spiral into disappointment and despair that lies in wait for all of us.' She smiled brightly at Sally and Polly. 'Just take it from me that everything will work out fine. Eventually. Sort of.' She frowned again and gave me a thoughtful look. 'You're going to need more than a standard portable door to get you into the Box Tunnel complex. There isn't an inch of that appalling place that isn't surrounded by serious levels of protection.'

'Any idea who's in charge these days?' I said.

Madam Osiris shook her head firmly. 'Just looking in the direction of Box Tunnel is enough to give me a headache.'

I had to raise an eyebrow. 'Why are you keeping a crystal eye on that place?'

'Because something is going on there!' snapped Madam Osiris. 'I don't need to be a major player to know that; the omens are kicking each other to death.' She broke off and looked uncertainly around the room, 'I'm sure I've got something here that would improve your chances, if I could only remember where I put it. Look at all this mess! I swear the pixies sneak in when I'm not looking and move things around.'

She went pottering around the room, picking things up and looking under them and occasionally making sounds of quiet disgust. Melody looked at me.

'Pixies?'

'Best not to ask,' I said.

'Gideon,' said Lex. 'Talk to me about the Box Tunnel complex. I seem to have missed a lot, and you know I hate being left out of things.'

I filled him in on the heist, and when I was done, Lex just nodded.

'I could use a good test of my abilities, to prove I'm myself again.' He looked at me steadily. 'You know what they say: if your horse throws you, shoot the ungrateful beast in the head and get a better mount. I need to throw myself headlong into crime and violence as soon as possible. So everyone will know the Damned is back.'

'It might be better if you took things easy for a while, darling,' said Sally. 'You nearly died . . .'

'Nearly doesn't cut it,' said Lex. 'I am Damned, which means I can do anything. And I will.' He turned to Polly. 'Why are you still a wolf?'

'Because your enemies are still looking for you,' she said sharply. 'I need to be prepared.'

'Good attitude,' said Lex. 'But the next time I tell you to stay away from somewhere, stay away.'

'Of course,' said Polly. And then she grinned wolfishly. 'I was right, though, wasn't I? Hogge was worth going after!'

'With extreme prejudice,' said Lex. 'And extra unnecessary violence on top.'

'We need to start working on a plan for the heist,' I said quickly. 'We don't want Hogge getting there first.'

Polly nodded at Madam Osiris, who was still busily searching through piles of things that seemed to constantly surprise her.

'Is it safe to talk freely?'

'I already know everything!' Madam Osiris said loudly, not turning around. 'I see the past, present and future – though not necessarily in that order. You have no idea how crowded it gets in my head sometimes, and that's with just me in here these days. Don't even get me started on alternative timelines.'

'She won't talk about anything she hears from us,' I said. 'Because that might interfere with the hold she thinks she has on Lex.'

'There are a few things I'd like to discuss about this heist, darlings,' said Sally. 'Starting with no money up front? Really?'

'If the Preserve holds even some of the things it's supposed to, this could be our biggest score ever,' I said.

'Can we trust Sharpe and Jacobi?' said Lex.

'We never trust anyone outside the crew,' I said.

'Damn right!' said Melody, with enough emphasis that we all looked at her. She shrugged quickly. 'Just saying . . .'

'Don't mind me, dears,' said Madam Osiris, kicking things out of her way and smiling when they squeaked. 'No one ever trusts me.'

'What about your toyboy?' said Melody.

'Jeremy will do as he's told,' said Madam Osiris. And something in the way she said that made the young man blush for a moment.

'It's obvious Sharpe was hiding things from us,' I said.

'Jacobi made the possessed pilot sound really dangerous,' said Melody. 'Sharpe didn't have much to say about that.'

'No,' I said. 'He didn't, did he?'

'So what are we going to do about this potentially deadly human-alien-ghost hybrid?' said Melody.

'Be very, very careful,' I said solemnly.

'I hate to keep coming back to this, but I'm going to because it is still freaking me out big time,' said Polly. 'Are you sure you can steal a ghost?'

'Please,' I said. 'I could steal your sense of direction, your favourite song and your birthday, and you wouldn't notice a thing.'

'The Preserve does sound intriguing,' said Sally. 'I can't wait to get in there and see what they've got tucked away. And walk away with it.'

'Is there a plan yet?' said Melody.

'I'm working on one,' I said.

Melody smiled sweetly. 'Work faster.'

'I'm assuming there will be the usual unpleasant security measures,' said Lex.

'Comes with the territory,' I said. 'You did say you wanted danger and excitement . . .'

'Will I get to hit people?' said Lex.

'Almost certainly.'

'I always wanted to hit a ghost,' said Lex, just a bit wistfully.

'That's the spirit,' I said.

'Any chance there might be live aliens inside the Preserve?' said Polly. 'Because I've always wanted to fight an alien.'

'That's my girl,' said Lex.

'Got it!' said Madam Osiris, and we all turned to look at her as she brandished a small glass bubble. 'This is what you need to get you to Box Tunnel. The Perfumed Highway! Not just another dimensional door, but a point-to-point delivery system that can't be intercepted or blocked! This is access to anywhere!' She paused, frowning. 'I don't normally keep the Perfumed Highway in stock – too expensive. But someone dropped me off a supply just recently, saying he thought I might need them later. And in my line of business, when someone warns you about the future, you listen. Now, just let me punch in the coordinates . . .' She pressed the glass bubble against her forehead, muttered under her breath and then handed the bubble over to me.

'There you go! That will drop you off somewhere on the outside of Box Tunnel Hill. Can't get you any closer, because then you'd trigger all kinds of alarms.'

'And the moment that happens, Mark Stone would know exactly where to look for us,' I said.

Madam Osiris looked at me sharply. 'He's involved in this? OK, that's it: I want all of you people out of my place right now!'

'Osiris . . .' said Jeremy.

She looked at him impatiently. 'What is it, sweetie?'

'Something's coming.'

We all turned to look at him. He was standing before the covered window, staring at the drapes as though he could see right through them.

'He's very sensitive,' said Madam Osiris. 'He notices things. What kind of thing are you talking about, Jeremy?'

'Something bad,' he said flatly. 'Dangerous people are heading this way. Some of them don't even feel like people. And, oh, they're so angry . . .'

Madam Osiris glared at Lex. 'This is all your fault! Your enemies have heard you're hurt, and they've tracked you here to take their revenge!'

Lex rose unhurriedly to his feet. He looked large and solid and ready to take on the world. The halos at his wrists blazed brightly.

'Let them come. Let them all come.'

'The Damned is back in the game, darlings!' Sally said happily.

Polly took up a position beside Lex, six feet and more of dark-furred werewolf.

'Growl,' she said.

'Oh, no,' Madam Osiris said quickly. 'You are not turning my place into a battlefield and making a mess of everything!'

'How would you tell the difference?' Melody said sweetly.

'They're getting closer,' said Jeremy. He hadn't taken his gaze away from the covered window. 'Really close.'

I moved in beside Madam Osiris. 'Just how reliable is he?'

'Very,' she said. 'He's my early warning system.'

'OK, everyone!' I said loudly. 'We are taking the Perfumed Highway to the Box Tunnel, right now!'

'I don't run from my enemies!' said the Damned.

'Smashing up Madam Osiris's place right after she saved your life would make for a very poor thank-you,' I said.

He nodded reluctantly.

'They should lose the trail once you've disappeared down the Perfumed Highway,' said Madam Osiris.

'Too late,' said Jeremy in an utterly calm voice. 'They're here.'

And, just like that, he changed into a huge humanoid wolf, a lean muscular figure covered in blond fur. I looked at Madam Osiris.

'Your new toyboy is a werewolf?'

She smiled. 'We all need someone to savage us in the nights.'

But Jeremy was looking at the other werewolf in the room. He grinned at Polly, and a long red tongue shot out to caress his fangs.

'See you after the fight?'

'Depends on how well you fight,' said Polly.

'You're such an animal.'

'You have no idea.'

The thick musk of flirting werewolves hung heavily on the air.

Madam Osiris stared at Polly and then at Jeremy. The crystal eyes often made her expression hard to read, but I had no difficulty this time. It was the look of a woman afraid she was losing her man to a younger woman, but still determined to fight for him. Jeremy's head came up, and he sniffed hard.

'They're here.'

The Dust Devils rose through the floor like so many grim grey ghosts. Human-shaped clouds of swirling dust held together by malign magics, they smelled like abandoned rooms and unswept corners. Sad remainders of lives no one cared about, harvested after their deaths and put to use. They started toward Lex, and Melody punched the nearest one in the face. Her fist sailed right through without even slowing, and she stumbled on, caught off balance. Another Dust Devil slammed into her like a battering ram. Melody cried out as she was thrown backwards but quickly regained her balance. The grey figure came after her and she struck out at it with both fists, but the grey ghost was only solid when it needed to hurt someone. The two werewolves charged right through the Dust Devils, preventing the indistinct figures from becoming solid. Both wolves sneezed heavily as they flailed viciously about them.

A door appeared in the far wall, and a dozen clockwork figures came striding through in perfect lockstep. The Automatic Assassins: pre-programmed clockwork automatons. Just wind them up and set them loose. No conscience, no remorse and no restraint. The perfect killing machines. I glared at the Damned.

'Is there anyone in the hidden world you haven't pissed off?'

'No one worth mentioning,' he said.

He put on his armour, and blinding light and bottomless darkness covered him from head to foot. An awful presence beat in the room, and everyone and everything hesitated where they were. Heaven and Hell had manifested in a small bed-sitting room, and even the clockwork killers and dusty remainders knew the bar had just been raised so far it was almost out of reach. That was why the Damned's enemies had sent such inhuman agents, who wouldn't stop even when reason told them to.

'Polly, Jeremy, Sally!' I yelled. 'You take the clockwork killers! Melody, don't give the Dust Devils a chance to reform! Lex, do something to close that door before more of the automatons turn up!'

The two werewolves hurled themselves at the clockwork figures and tore them apart with vicious fang and claw work. Metal pieces flew through the air as Polly and Jeremy reduced the Automatic Assassins to so much scrap metal. Sally concentrated on the figures they missed, switching one clockwork part for another until the automatons self-destructed. Lex slammed the dimensional door shut and set his armoured shoulder against it. Something hammered heavily on the other side, trying to force it open.

Melody charged back and forth, throwing herself through one dusty figure after another so they never got the chance to become solid and a threat. But the effort was taking it out of her. She was already breathing hard, and it wouldn't be long before she was forced to slow down, and then the Dust Devils would close in on her.

I was still working on a plan when a dozen men with the same face came crashing through the ceiling, abseiling down on invisible ropes. The Borden Brigade were mass-produced muscle, cloned from an original who stayed safely at home and sent his other selves out to do his dirty work. Supernaturally enhanced in the strength and speed department, the clones burned through their lives in a hurry, but it was easy enough for the original to whip up another batch.

'Look what you did to my ceiling, you bastards!' Madam Osiris shouted, and one of the clones stopped to address her.

'Awfully sorry, old thing. But we do have a job to do, so please withdraw to a safe distance and allow us to get on with things, there's a dear.'

Madam Osiris punched him in the throat so hard I heard cartilage break. The clone dropped to the floor, and she stamped on his head. The other clones ignored them and headed straight for Lex, who was still holding the dimensional door shut.

I looked quickly around to check Polly, Sally and Jeremy were still reducing the Automatic Assassins to their various bits and pieces, and then produced my skeleton key. I pointed it at the Dust Devils swarming around Melody like angry clouds and unlocked the forces that held the grey ghosts together. Just like that, every single one of them collapsed into patches of slowly falling dust. Melody glared at me.

'I didn't need your help!'

'Of course not,' I said. 'I was just worried one of them might get past you and come for me.'

She nodded quickly, gathered her strength and hit the Borden Brigade from behind as they battered away at the Damned, unable to make any impression on his armour. Melody rabbit-punched the first clone she came to, kidney-punched the next and kicked the feet out from under a third, but they were all up and at her again in a moment. The Damned saw she was in trouble and moved forward to help. The dimensional door started to open behind him.

'Stay where you are, Lex!' I yelled. 'We can't risk any more of the Automatic Assassins getting in!'

The clones only came in batches, but there was no limit to the clockwork killers. The Damned put his armoured shoulder to the door and forced it shut again. The heavy wood split from top to bottom. The Damned ignored the clones scrabbling at his armour and turned his featureless face to me.

'If the door collapses, we're in trouble.'

I nodded quickly. Even the Damned in his armour could be swept away by enough bodies acting at once. I turned to Melody. Clones were swarming around her, easily avoiding her increasingly desperate blows and kicks. I started toward her, but Madam Osiris stopped me with a hand on my shoulder.

'I'll handle this. Lex, get out of the way.'

The Damned shot me a look and then stepped to one side. The door slammed all the way open, revealing rank upon rank of Automatic Assassins. Madam Osiris took a deep breath and raised her voice.

'Protection Protocol Blue Silver!'

Her crystal eyes blazed fiercely, and the door slammed shut and disappeared. Madam Osiris shot me a knowing look.

'I've still got it . . .'

'Only because I gave it to you,' I said.

I went to help Melody. The Borden Brigade turned as one to face me, and then they all aged several decades in a few seconds and dropped to the floor. They'd used up their entire lives fighting us. Melody stared at the fallen figures, breathing heavily, and then kicked a few in the head just to be sure. I turned to check out Polly, Sally and Jeremy, but they were standing easily together, surrounded by broken clockwork.

The Dust Devils were dispersed, the Automatic Assassins had been reduced to their component parts, and the Borden Brigade were just so many shrivelled mummies on the floor.

It was suddenly very still and very quiet in the small bed-sitting room. Madam Osiris looked at the holes in her ceiling and shook her head.

'Time for another moonlit flit . . .'

Polly and Jeremy high-fived each other with their hairy hands and grinned fiercely. Polly moved in close to sniff at Jeremy's face, and if he'd had a tail, I think it would have been wagging. Madam Osiris looked at the two werewolves for a long moment and then clapped her hands loudly.

'That's it! I want everyone out of here! As long as the Damned is hanging around, the bad guys will just keep coming. What we saw was merely the opening act; the heavy-duty monsters are still on their way.'

I shook my head solemnly. 'There's no need for us to rush off.'

Madam Osiris glared at me. 'What?'

'You once asked me the best way to protect yourself,' I said. 'And I presented you with the Protection Protocol. So I know this whole room has been taken out of Space and Time for at least an hour. Plenty of time to sit down with my crew and work out how we're going to deal with the security meas-ures inside the Box Tunnel complex. And the Preserve. You and Jeremy find somewhere quiet to sit and let us get on with it, and we'll be out of your hair before you know it.'

Madam Osiris glowered at Jeremy. 'Never let anyone do you a favour. It'll always come back to bite you on the arse. What did I do to deserve you, Gideon?'

'You were probably very bad in a previous life,' said Melody.

Madam Osiris started to say something and then broke off as she realized Jeremy had turned back into his human self and was now entirely naked.

'Put some clothes on! We've got company!' Madam Osiris stopped again as Polly changed back into her equally naked human form. 'Both of you stand right where you are until I find you something.'

She quickly came up with a shabby brown dressing gown for Jeremy. He shrugged it on with complete indifference and had to be reminded to do up the belt to close it at the front.

Madam Osiris then produced an emerald-green silk kimono for Polly, who made happy admiring noises as she slipped into it.

'I want that back when you're done with it, my girl,' said Madam Osiris. 'And dry-cleaned if you get blood on it, which, knowing Gideon, you probably will.'

She then bustled around the room, pulling an assortment of chairs out of the general chaos and arranging them around a circular table I would have sworn wasn't there a moment before. I sat down with my crew, and Madam Osiris sat on the bed with Jeremy.

'Thanks for the support,' I said.

Madam Osiris sniffed loudly. 'Like I had a choice.'

'You know, you are welcome to join us on the heist,' I said. 'There should be enough goodies for everyone.'

'I would rather bite my own head off,' Madam Osiris said flatly. 'Even if we could get in and out of the Preserve with all our important bits still attached, I do not want Mark Stone coming after me.' Jeremy started to say something and then stopped as she glared at him. 'You're just a wolf; he's a hellhound.'

I turned back to my crew. They looked at me expectantly, but I had some other business to attend to first. I looked steadily at Melody.

'Take off the wig.'

'What wig?' said Melody.

'You've proved very useful so far,' I said steadily. 'But I need Annie's expertise to help put my plan together.'

She stared right back at me. 'Who is this Annie you keep going on about? I never even heard of her!'

She realized everyone else was staring at her and glared defiantly around the table. Madam Osiris stirred on the bed.

'Gideon . . . How long has this been going on?'

'Just today,' I said. 'Can you help?'

'None of my other selves ever denied each other's existence,' said Madam Osiris. 'They just hated everyone else's guts and refused to talk to each other.'

Melody jumped to her feet and stepped back from the table. I stood up to face her, and she held herself like a fighter waiting for the opening bell.

'Don't look at me like that! There's nothing wrong with me!'

'Take it easy, darling,' Sally said carefully. 'We just want to help.'

'We're all here for you,' said Polly.

'Whoever that is,' said Lex.

'Are you?' said Melody.

And while she was busy glaring around the table, I ripped the black wig off her head.

'Sorry,' I said. 'But I need Annie.'

The woman in the grey catsuit cried out as though I'd hit her, and then her whole posture changed as she seemed to shrink in on herself. Her face went through a series of subtle changes until Annie's features emerged. She straightened up, put a hand to her face and then ran it slowly over her blonde buzz cut, before finally turning to look at me.

'I'm back,' she said.

I started to hand her the wig, then thought better of it and tossed it on to the chest of drawers.

'I didn't know what else to do,' I said. 'How much do you remember, about being Melody?'

'It feels like I've been dreaming,' Annie said slowly.

'Do you need me to bring you up to speed?'

'No. I know what the score is.'

'Why did you want to be Melody Mead in the first place?'

Annie frowned. 'I don't remember. She's an odd choice. I haven't felt the need to be her in ages.'

'Maybe it's the wig!' Sally said brightly. We all looked at her, and she shrugged. 'Maybe the wig is possessed?'

I didn't argue. I'd encountered stranger things. Annie shook her head firmly.

'I've used it often enough before, without any problems.'

'Oh, poo,' said Sally. 'I was so sure I was being helpful . . .'

'Could this be some form of outside attack?' said Lex.

I wasn't surprised his mind had gone there. The Damned always thought in terms of attacks from outside.

'I don't think so,' said Annie.

She seated herself at the table, and after a moment I did, too.

'Let's concentrate on the plan,' said Annie. 'I'll feel better once I'm doing something.'

I looked to Madam Osiris. 'I need access to the information underworld. Can we use your big crystal ball?'

Madam Osiris sniffed haughtily. 'That's just for the punters.' She raised her voice. 'Activate portal, general access agreed.'

A rather snotty voice rose out of the table. 'Are you sure? These are not reputable people.'

'Of course I'm sure!' said Madam Osiris. 'Just do as you're told and get on with it.'

The tabletop glowed with a shimmering silver light, and the voice continued in a more conciliatory manner.

'What do you need to know?'

'Is this going to be like Sidney the talking mirror?' Sally said cheerfully. 'I like Sidney. Mostly.'

The tabletop didn't actually sniff loudly but sounded as though it wanted to.

'Oh, please, those things are so last century.'

'I prefer to get my information from people,' said Lex. 'You know where you are with people. If you hit them hard enough.'

'We don't have time for you to beat the truth out of the entire criminal underworld,' I said. 'Table, give us whatever you have on the Box Tunnel complex, including the Preserve.'

A raging avalanche of files and images flashed across the glowing tabletop, come and gone so quickly I could barely register them, but I could feel the information sinking into my mind and making itself at home. There was a lot more than I'd expected, including not just official information but insider gossip and recent conspiracy chatter. The table was accessing a lot of seriously restricted materials; I just hoped no one at the other end knew what was going on.

Slowly, piece by piece, a plan came together.

The images slammed to a halt. I sat back in my chair, closed my eyes and massaged my aching temples. I'd absorbed an unhealthy amount of information in a really short time, and my mind was trying to decide whether that was a good thing. I opened my eyes and found my crew looking at me blankly.

'Did something just happen there?' said Annie. 'Only, if it did, I'm pretty sure the rest of us missed it.'

I looked around at my crew. 'You didn't see any of what the table showed me?'

They all shook their heads emphatically. Madam Osiris smiled at me.

'My table likes you.'

I nodded, just a bit shakily.

'You can shut it down now.'

'Glad to have been of service!' the table said brightly.

'Oh, shut up,' said Madam Osiris.

'You don't appreciate me,' said the table.

The silver light snapped off, and my crew looked at me expectantly. I was getting a little tired of always having to be the man with the plan. It might be nice if, just occasionally, someone else would volunteer to do the heavy lifting. Not that I'd trust any plan this bunch came up with.

'Let's start with Box Tunnel,' I said. 'After the original complex was emptied and shut down, another underground city was established, only buried even deeper. Because who'd look for a secret city under a secret city? This new complex includes the Preserve, which was somehow transferred complete and intact. The underground city is packed full of things that don't officially exist, including a whole lot of alien technology. Which strongly suggests the new people in charge . . . are Black Heir.'

'Hey, I've heard of them!' said Jeremy, paying attention for the first time. 'They are all about sticking it to the aliens! I mean, seriously hardcore!'

'You've been surfing the table again, haven't you?' said Madam Osiris. Jeremy just grinned at her.

'He's quite right,' I said. 'When the SAS have a headache, and the Men in Black don't want to know, that's when Black Heir get sent in to stamp all over everything. They cherry-pick the good stuff for themselves and destroy everything else.'

'What about the aliens?' said Polly.

'They tend not to survive close encounters with Black Heir,' I said.

'Told you,' said Jeremy. 'Bad guys!'

'That's not always a good thing, sweetie,' said Madam Osiris.

'Could Mark Stone be working for Black Heir?' said Annie.

'Wouldn't surprise me,' I said. 'Now, all the approaches to

Box Tunnel Hill are monitored by armed guards, and we're bound to run into more inside the complex.'

'How are we going to get past them?' said Annie.

'Put Lex out in front,' said Sally. 'The rest of us can hide behind him and listen to the bullets bouncing off his armour.'

'We can't be sure what kind of weapons the guards have,' I said carefully.

'I am armoured by Heaven and Hell,' said Lex.

'That doesn't cover everything,' I said.

'Couldn't we disguise ourselves as official visitors?' said Polly.

'There aren't many authorized visitors,' I said. 'And they get very thoroughly checked before they're allowed in, to make sure they are who they're claiming to be.'

'So how are we getting in?' said Annie.

'The secret tunnel Professor Jacobi told us about,' I said. 'It hasn't been used in so long that hopefully the new bosses won't know about it.'

'I know I'm new to this crew,' said Polly. 'But I can already see a whole bunch of things that could go wrong.'

'Burglary isn't a science,' I said. 'There always has to be room for creative improvisation. Try not to worry about it.'

'Trying really hard,' Polly said sweetly.

'Once we're inside the complex, our passwords and security overrides should shut down the surveillance systems. If that doesn't work, Annie will use her gift to charm the mechanisms into seeing things our way.'

Sally pulled a face at Annie. 'Making machines fall in love with you is definitely icky, darling.'

Annie smiled for the first time. 'Don't knock it till you've tried it.'

'If her charm doesn't work, we could be in serious trouble,' said Polly. 'If we leave any record of our visit, Black Heir will never stop coming after us.'

'Relax,' I said. 'I didn't just steal a portable door at the Thieves Bazaar; I also helped myself to enough false faces for all of us.'

Sally clapped her hands delightedly. 'You really do think ahead, darling!'

'That's what makes me the man with the plan.'

I dropped several pink blobs on to the table and gestured for everyone to help themselves.

'What is it with the Thieves Bazaar and blobs?' said Sally. 'Hey, these things look just like the chewy pink candies I used to love as a child.'

'I can't believe I'm having to say this, but do *not* put the false faces in your mouth,' I said. 'If you swallow one, we don't have time to wait for them to re-emerge.'

'Where do these things come from?' said Polly, sniffing thoughtfully at hers.

I shrugged. 'Ask a dozen different people and you'll end up with thirteen different answers.'

Lex squeezed his blob between his fingers and studied it suspiciously. 'How does it work?'

'Haven't you ever used a disguise?' said Annie.

'No,' said Lex. 'I want my enemies to know who's killing them.'

I rolled my blob back and forth between my palms until it was soft and pliable, and then slapped it against my forehead.

'OK . . .' said Sally. 'You look just like you did before.'

'But any surveillance system will only see a blank, featureless mask,' I said.

'Sneaky,' said Polly. 'I like it.'

They all took it in turns to flatten the false faces in place, and after a moment the blobs disappeared. I could still feel mine, like a cold hand pressed against my forehead, but that would pass.

'What about the guards?' said Annie.

'They'll see a blank face, too.'

'Won't they just open fire, when presented with an invasion of the faceless people?'

'They'd shoot at strangers anyway,' I said.

'We can always line up and hide behind Lex,' said Polly.

He looked at her. 'Whose side are you on?'

Sally put a hand on his arm. 'If you don't feel up to being shot at, perhaps you should stay behind, darling.'

Lex looked at her until she took her hand away.

'What kind of traps and pitfalls should we be expecting?'

said Polly, in her best *I am changing the subject* voice.
'Weapons systems or living things?'

'Yes,' I said. 'You can sniff them out, or Annie can charm
the traps into staying shut. If that doesn't work, you're up,
Lex.'

He nodded. 'Looking forward to it.'

'The table showed me floor plans for the entire complex,'
I said. 'I've worked out an only slightly roundabout route that
should allow us to avoid most things.' I stopped and looked
around the table. 'My plan comes to a sudden halt the moment
we reach the Preserve, which is designed to keep a great many
dangerous things from escaping. So strict rule, people: once
we're inside the Preserve, *no one is to touch anything without
asking me first.*'

'Why is everyone looking at me?' said Sally.

'Now,' I said. 'We come to the ghost. It could be the restless spirit of the dead pilot or the last remnant of the alien
hybrid.'

'Assuming it is just a ghost,' said Polly, 'and I'm having
trouble believing that is the less scary option, are you positive
you can steal it?'

'Why does everyone keep asking me that?' I said. 'Come
on, it's not rocket surgery. You trap a ghost by using spirit
bottles, words of binding, or by allowing one of us to become
temporarily possessed so we can smuggle the ghost out.'

Sally put a hand in the air. 'Can I just make it extremely
clear that I am not in any way volunteering to do that?'

'What she said,' growled Polly. 'Only with even more
emphasis.'

'That would be a last resort,' I said reassuringly. 'You can
put your hand down now, Sally. What plan we eventually use
will depend on what kind of ghost it turns out to be.'

'But have you ever actually stolen a ghost before?' said
Annie.

'Sort of,' I said. And then looked around the table in a way
that made it clear I wasn't disposed to discuss the matter.
Everyone else stared right back at me in a way that made it
equally clear that there would be more discussion about this,
at some future point.

'Apart from the ghost,' said Annie, 'how are we going to deal with all the dangerous things in the Preserve?'

'By leaving them strictly alone,' I said. 'We only steal things that won't fight back.'

'Any particular ones we should steer clear of?' said Sally.

'We need to be extremely cautious around Catherine Cairne, the Sleeping AI,' I said. 'She used to be just another scientist back in the fifties, until an alien computer downloaded itself into her head. Then she became such a threat that her own people had no choice but to subdue her. She's been in an induced coma ever since, in a combination coffin and support system. Apparently, it would be a very bad idea to wake her up. So let's try really hard not to do that.'

'But what could she do that's so dangerous?' said Sally. 'I mean, honestly, darling, she's only a woman with a bit more intelligence in her head. I can see how that might make some military men nervous, but . . .'

'It's alien information,' I said. 'Even in her sleep Catherine Cairne can answer any question put to her, but she always presents her answer in a form guaranteed to do the most damage to the questioner. And if anyone asks her the wrong question, she will rise from her coffin and lay waste to the Preserve and everyone in it.'

'What is the wrong question?' said Polly.

'No one knows,' I said. 'So . . .'

'Don't talk to the nasty alien computer person,' said Sally. 'Good safety tip there, darlings.'

'I've made a list of items to avoid,' I said. 'And another of what to grab and run off with. Don't get the lists confused. Any questions . . . no . . . good . . . let's get moving.'

Annie turned to Madam Osiris. 'Where is this Perfumed Highway going to drop us off, at Box Tunnel?'

'Somewhere on the outside of the hill,' said Madam Osiris.

'Outside?' said Polly. 'Where all the armed soldiers are lying in wait?'

'You're not bothered by a few guns, are you?' said Lex.

Polly glared at him. 'Lead bullets can't kill me, but they still hurt like hell. And I've been through enough of that for one day.'

Lex patted her arm. 'I will never let anything like that happen to you again.'

'I know both of you have been through a lot,' I said. 'I would like to give you time to rest and recover, but we have to do this before Hogge can put his own crew together.'

'You put your heist at risk, to save Polly and me,' said Lex. 'I haven't forgotten.'

'You're crew,' I said. 'That makes you family.'

'I'm in,' said Lex.

'Me, too,' said Polly. 'Let's do this thing.'

'Yay for the crew!' said Sally, punching the air.

'I can't go with you as me,' said Annie.

We all turned to look at her.

'You need someone who can fight and deal with dangerous artefacts,' she said flatly. 'That isn't me.'

'You don't have access to your wardrobe to create another persona,' I said. 'And I'm not taking Melody.'

'She's all I have,' said Annie.

She jumped up from her chair and lunged for the chest of drawers. The rest of us had only just got to our feet when she snatched up the black wig and clapped it on her head. Her stance and face changed in a moment, and, just like that, she was Melody Mead again. She smiled at us defiantly.

'I'm back! And don't even think about trying to get rid of me again!'

I gestured urgently for the others to stay where they were, and then moved cautiously forward. I was ready to tear the wig off, if that was what it took to get Annie back, but Melody stopped me with a look that said she'd fight me if I tried.

'You're going to need me if it all goes wrong inside the Preserve!' Melody said quickly. 'Lex and Polly might be better fighters, but they can't bring the crafty like I can.'

'She has a point,' said Lex. 'She can do things that Annie couldn't.'

'Annie isn't crazy,' I said.

'I'm not crazy,' said Melody. 'I'm just focused.'

'Who are you?' I said. 'Really?'

She met my gaze steadily. 'It's me, Gideon. I'm your Mel.'

I hadn't been expecting that. The calm certainty in her voice, the look in her eyes . . . And she was right. I did need her. I just had to hope I could coax Annie back out again when this was over.

'All right,' I said. 'You're in.'

The rest of the crew looked at me like I was the crazy one, but then the tabletop blazed with silver light as the voice of Sidney the talking mirror burst out of it.

'Heads up and pay attention! Every nasty thing in the world is heading your way, right now, in a really bad mood!'

'Sidney?' I said. 'How did you get into the table?'

'Hacked its operating system,' he said smugly. 'Wasn't difficult. These new systems think they're so smart . . .'

'How did you get past my Protection Protocols?' said Madam Osiris.

'Oh, please. Who do you think created them in the first place?' said Sidney. 'Now, stop wittering and listen! You have to get out of there, right now, because every single enemy Lex ever made is about to come battering at your doors!'

'All of them?' said Lex. He didn't sound concerned, more flattered.

'I cannot believe how many top-rank magical operators you have seriously pissed off in your time,' said Sidney. 'They held back before this because they were scared of your armour, but now word is out that you're vulnerable—'

'I am not vulnerable!' said Lex.

'They don't know that!' Sidney said loudly. 'They've tracked you to Madam Osiris's current hidey-hole, and are ready to descend on you like the wrath of Beelzebub.'

'Let them come,' said Lex, smiling. 'Let them all come.'

'This isn't the time to prove you're still the biggest dog on the block,' I said. 'You saw what just three of your minor enemies did to this room. Imagine what the really bad guys will do when they show up.'

'Then go,' said Lex. 'I can handle this.'

'No, you can't, darling,' said Sally. 'Not on the best day you ever had, which this definitely isn't. If you stay, we stay with you.'

'What she said,' said Polly.

Madam Osiris came over to join us, with Jeremy hovering at her side.

'Go,' she said. 'The Protection Protocols will disguise your destination.'

'Come with us,' I said.

'No,' Madam Osiris said flatly. 'This is my place, and I will not be driven out of it.'

'We can't leave you here on your own,' I said.

'She won't be alone,' said Jeremy.

Madam Osiris turned to look at him. 'You don't have to stay.'

Jeremy smiled. 'Of course I do.'

And then the whole room shuddered, as something beat savagely against the Protocol's barriers, trying to force its way in. Furniture danced across the floor, and the table exploded, cutting off Sidney's voice in mid-rant. Bottles fell from the shelves to break and shatter on the floor, and the Baron Samedi skeleton hid its face in its hands. Lex glared about him, the halos blazing fiercely at his wrists, needing to prove, if only to himself, that he was still the man he used to be before Hogge and his people broke him. Sally and Polly closed in on either side of him.

'You stay, we stay,' said Sally.

'All the way,' said Polly.

'Damn right,' said Melody.

Lex looked to me, and I nodded. He turned to Madam Osiris.

'I can't stay and risk my friends,' he said. 'That would be selfish.'

He nodded to me, and I crushed the glass bubble in my hand. A thick purple mist boiled up to envelop me and my crew. Madam Osiris and Jeremy stood well back. The mist grew thicker, and my crew and I began to fade away.

The last thing I saw was a great crack forming in the damaged ceiling, and a terrible light falling through as something from outside looked in. A triumphant roar shook the room. Madam Osiris glared up into the crack, her crystal eyes blazing with their own terrible light. Wild energies crackled around her upraised hands, as Madam Osiris came into her own at last.

Jeremy stood snarling at her side, every inch the werewolf. Ready to fight anything that threatened the woman he had chosen to stand with.

And then the mists of the Perfumed Highway rose, and we were gone.

SIX

To Make God Smile, Have a Plan

The expected grassy hillside of Box Tunnel turned out to be conspicuous by its absence. Instead, we arrived inside a narrow tunnel with walls of rough earth and no sign of support. The only light came from the Perfumed Highway's glowing purple mists, which were already beginning to die down and disperse. But as they started to ebb away, a single light flickered on above us, providing a pool of flat yellow illumination. Rather than meet the accusing eyes of my crew, I gave all my attention to the nearest wall.

'This tunnel wasn't made with machinery or even tools; it looks more like it was burrowed out. By some . . . huge living thing.'

'I want to go home,' said Sally. 'Right now, if not sooner.'

'Relax,' I said. 'There's nothing recent about this. Whatever made this tunnel, it all happened a long time ago.'

'But what kind of huge living thing are we talking about?' said Melody. 'Monstrous worms, killer moles? What kind of things did they have in the complex, back in the day?'

'More importantly, are any of them still around?' said Sally. 'And ready to come charging back down the tunnel in search of a snack?'

Polly raised her wolf head and sniffed thoughtfully. 'Nothing has passed this way in a long time. But I really don't like the quality of this air. We should get moving.'

Lex gestured at the overhead light. 'Doesn't that mean someone already knows we're here?'

'More likely it was just activated by our presence,' said Melody.

I jumped, just a little, as the last of the purple mists vanished and the glass bubble reappeared in my hand, restored and intact and ready to be used again. Madam Osiris must have paid extra for the luxury package. I tucked the bubble away in a handy pocket.

'Since no one else is talking about the elephant in the tunnel, I'll throw my hat into the ring,' said Sally. 'Why aren't we outside on the hill, where we were supposed to arrive?'

'You mean in plain sight, where the armed guards could get a clear shot at us?' I said.

'Not necessarily,' said Sally. 'But really, where the hell are we?'

'I think we're inside the secret tunnel the young scientists used when they felt like sneaking out for a bit of fun,' I said. 'Which means the Perfumed Highway is an even better delivery system than Madam Osiris knew. It brought us where we needed to be, rather than where we asked for.'

'I don't think I approve of things with a mind of their own,' said Lex. 'It can lead to arguments.'

'Just think of it as the Perfumed Highway being very thorough,' I said. 'Because I am all for appearing in a place where people aren't going to use us for target practice.'

'It gets my vote,' said Polly.

I looked at her steadily. 'Can I just ask: why are you still wearing your kimono, even though you're full wolf?'

Polly glanced down at the green silk gown. 'Because it suits me.'

'It's a style thing, darling,' said Sally. 'You wouldn't understand.'

'Probably not,' I said.

I took out my compass, checked the needle and pointed down the tunnel.

'This way to the inner door, people.'

'Not to rain on our own parade,' said Sally, 'but what if our presence triggered a silent alarm inside the complex? I can't believe they'd leave an entrance tunnel unmonitored. People like us might break in.'

'There are no surveillance systems here,' said Melody. 'My gift for charming machines makes me very aware of their presence.'

'Spooky . . .' said Sally.

'The young scientists wouldn't have wanted their superiors

to know what they were up to,' I said. 'I've no doubt they took precautions.'

Polly frowned, which was a worrying thing to see on the face of a werewolf.

'But if this is an old tunnel, doesn't that mean it connects to the old underground city, rather than the new one?'

'Good point,' I said. 'But Sharpe wouldn't have told us about this unless it could take us where we need to be.'

'Can we get a move on?' said Lex. 'I didn't come all this way just to hang around in Watership Down.'

'He loves that book,' Sally said confidingly. 'He likes me to read it to him while we're in bed.'

'Far too much information,' I said.

We set off along the tunnel. I put Polly in the lead, in the hope her enhanced senses would warn us of any dangers up ahead. And because if there were any, it would help if the first thing they encountered was a very large werewolf. Lex stuck close behind her, with Sally tucked in at his side. They were all being very protective of each other, while trying not to be too obvious about it.

Melody strode cheerfully along beside me. I still didn't understand why she insisted on being Melody and claiming she'd never heard of Annie. Something was very wrong there, and it worried me that I had no idea what it was.

I hate it when real-life problems intrude on a heist.

'I hope Madam Osiris will be all right,' said Polly, after a while. 'I didn't like abandoning her to face the bad guys alone.'

'She had Jeremy,' said Sally.

'Even so,' said Polly.

'Don't worry,' I said. 'Madam Osiris will hold her ground just long enough to throw the bad guys off our trail, and then make a swift exit with her own Perfumed Highway.'

'I thought she was very brave,' Sally said firmly. 'I never knew she cared so much about us.'

'She doesn't,' I said, just as firmly. 'That defiant last stand was all about making sure Lex felt obligated to her.'

'There's more to Madam Osiris than meets the eye,' said

Melody. 'But then there would have to be. How powerful is she, really?'

'I don't think anyone knows,' I said. 'That's kind of the point. She likes to play down her abilities, so her enemies will underestimate her.'

'And her friends?' said Melody.

'Well,' I said, 'that goes without saying.'

The tunnel turned out to be a lot longer than I expected. The overhead lights turned themselves on and off as we progressed, so we were always plodding along in a small pool of light surrounded by darkness. I think we were all a bit relieved when Polly finally came to a halt.

'There's a door.'

'Are you sure?' said Melody, scowling into the dark.

'Trust the nose,' said Polly. 'The nose knows.'

The door turned out to be a featureless steel slab with no handle – just a big blocky keypad with a thick layer of dust covering the numbers.

'What is this?' said Sally. 'Eighties retro chic?'

Melody leaned in for a closer look. 'This is a dimensional door.'

'Of course,' I said. 'Designed to deliver people to wherever they needed to be, as long as they enter the right access codes.'

'Did the table give you the numbers?' said Melody.

'No,' I said. 'Probably because I didn't know enough to ask for them. But I do have several security overrides, courtesy of Professors Sharpe and Jacobi.'

I carefully punched them in, one after another; none of them worked.

'If the higher-ups forgot about the tunnel, they might have forgotten about upgrading the door,' said Melody.

I nodded stiffly. 'The thought had occurred to me.'

'So how are we going to get in?' said Polly.

'Why are you still being a wolf?' I said.

'Because I have a really bad feeling about this,' said Polly.

'It has been that kind of a day,' said Lex.

'Melody,' I said, 'you're up. Charm this keypad and get the door on our side.'

Melody fixed the door with her most compelling gaze. Her gift was just a love charm that had gone wrong, because she hadn't thought to steal the instruction manual along with the charm. It made machines fall in love with her and eager to do whatever it took to please her. The keypad suddenly ran through a series of numbers, and the door made a polite chiming noise as it swung back.

'Every time I see it, that really weirds me out,' growled Polly.

'Love makes the world go round,' Melody said solemnly.

Beyond the door was nothing but an impenetrable darkness. We all studied it carefully.

'I don't know how much I trust this door,' said Sally, not moving an inch.

'Trust the gift,' said Melody. 'I can feel the door smiling.'

Sally shook her head. 'And she thinks that's a good thing . . .'

'Hush,' said Melody. 'It can hear you.'

She strode forward into the darkness, and after a moment we followed her in.

We emerged into a light so bright we all had to stop and blink heavily. I was braced for unfriendly guards and shrieking alarms, but everything was very still and very quiet. When my eyes had cleared enough for me to take a good look around, I could see why.

We'd arrived on an empty platform, in the middle of a huge underground railway station, inside a massive cavern carved out of the bedrock under Box Tunnel Hill. Endless rows of fluorescent lights hung down from the cavern ceiling, spreading a harsh, unflattering light across a series of platforms, each with their own trains and carriages. There was no one around. We had the whole place to ourselves. When I checked out the display boards, none of them were showing any destinations.

I glanced behind me. The dimensional door had disappeared, as though it had never been there.

'Why is there a railway station?' said Melody.

'The complex is an underground city,' I said patiently. 'Covering God knows how many square miles. How else were they going to get around? Golf carts?'

'But where is everyone?' said Sally. 'I mean, yes, I'm happy we're not being yelled at or shot at, but I wasn't expecting a ghost town.'

'Something bad happened here,' said Polly. 'And not that long ago, because I'm still picking up faint scents of panic and alarm and deep unhappiness. I don't know where everyone went, but whatever it was scared the piss out of them.'

'Any blood?' I said. 'Traces of violence?'

She shook her head.

'There's a café over there,' said Sally. 'Shall we take a look?'

'You can't want more tea,' I said.

She glared at me. 'People talk in cafés. They discuss things. They might have left a note or a clue.'

'Of course,' I said. 'After you.'

'Hell with that,' said Sally. She flashed a smile at Lex. 'After you, darling.'

'But no armour,' I said quickly. 'Let's not start something if we don't have to.'

'Of course,' said Lex.

The café was modern, comfortable and completely deserted. Whatever went wrong, it must have hit the place without any warning. Food lay half eaten on plates, drinks had been left unfinished or spilled across the tables, and several chairs had been overturned.

'Very *Marie Celeste*,' said Polly.

'These people didn't just leave,' said Melody. 'They dropped everything and bolted for the door.'

'Could the ghost have broken out of the Preserve?' said Lex.

'I'm not smelling anything here apart from people,' said Polly. 'Very upset people.'

Sally shuddered delicately. 'It feels like we missed something, darlings – and not by much.'

'We need access to the main computer systems,' I said. 'The complex must have a record of events, right up to the point where it all went pear-shaped.'

'You could always try the Manager's Office,' said Sally, pointing to a door with a frosted window and a sign saying *Manager's Office*.

I let her lead the way. Inside, papers were scattered every-where, as though they just didn't matter any more. I sat down before one of the computers and fired it up, only to discover it was still password-protected. Melody cleared her throat in a significant sort of way, and I stood up so she could take my place. It only took her a moment to charm the computer into opening up.

'Ask me anything, dear,' said a cool, calm female voice. 'I can deny you nothing.'

'What happened?' said Melody. 'Why did everyone leave in such a hurry?'

'The order was given to evacuate the complex,' said the computer. 'Because the nuclear countdown has started.'

'*What?*' I said. Followed closely by '*Why?*'

'To destroy the Preserve and everything it contains,' said the computer. 'That is Standing Order Number One, and it has been ever since Black Heir moved the Preserve here. I did warn them against that, but no one ever listens to me.'

'How long do we have, before the nuke blows everything into radioactive dust?' said Melody.

'Oh, ages yet,' said the computer.

'Define ages,' said Melody.

'You have a little over twelve hours until detonation.'

'Why such a long countdown?' said Sally. 'Not that I'm complaining, you understand.'

'To give all personnel a reasonable chance to reach a safe distance,' said the computer. 'The threat from the Preserve was considered to be great, but not imminent. Otherwise, Black Heir would have just set off the nuke, and to hell with everyone here. Because they're like that.'

'Twelve hours is more than enough time for us to get to the Preserve, and get the job done,' I said, looking steadily at each crew member in turn. 'It's just another deadline. We can do deadlines.' And then I stopped and frowned. 'No guards, no one and nothing left in the complex to get in our way . . . It's almost as though someone is looking out for us.'

Lex raised an eyebrow. 'A nuclear bomb on a countdown is someone's idea of being helpful?'

'It is, if you think about it,' I said. 'All the expected obstacles between us and the Preserve have been removed. And once the nuke blows, it will be impossible for anyone to tell what might have been removed from the Preserve.'

'Why would anyone go to such lengths to help us?' said Melody.

'Because they really want us to steal the ghost,' I said.

'Are we looking at Sharpe or Jacobi, as the Man Behind Everything?' said Sally.

'More likely, someone further in the background,' I said.

'You think we're being played,' said Lex.

'Wouldn't surprise me.'

'What do we do now?' said Polly. 'And I mean right now, because I do not want to be here one minute longer than necessary.'

'We concentrate on the heist,' I said firmly. 'Once we're inside the Preserve, and face to face with the ghost, I'll figure out how to remove it, and then we will get the hell out of Dodge and hand the ghost over to Sharpe. Or whoever's pulling his strings.'

'Not forgetting to help ourselves to as many goodies as we can carry out of the Preserve,' said Sally.

'Well obviously,' I said.

Melody persuaded the computer to program one of the trains to take us to the Preserve. Instead of the stockpiled steam trains I'd been expecting, it turned out to be an elegant silver-bullet train, with no windows on the carriages and not even a windscreen on the engine, which was just a bit worrying. The door to the driver's compartment was open, so we all packed ourselves into the cramped space.

'Anyone know how to drive a train?' said Sally.

'I do,' said the computer's voice from the controls. 'So no one is to touch *anything*. Go sit in the next carriage, and I'll get you as close to the Preserve as I can without actually jumping the train off the tracks. Because that would be bad.'

Lights flickered across the controls, and a loud humming shook the train. The next carriage turned out to be surprisingly well appointed, and just like on the London Underground, there was a map showing all the various lines and destinations. They were helpfully colour-coded, but not in a way that made any sense, so it took me a while to figure out which line led to the Preserve. It didn't help that Melody kept peering over my shoulder and being helpful. I finally located the Preserve station at the end of a long separate line with no other stopping points along the way.

'The train stops well short of the Preserve,' I said. 'We'll have to walk the rest of the way.'

'How far?' said Lex.

'Hard to tell,' I said. 'The Preserve is right on the outskirts of the complex: as far away from everyone else as they could manage while still being able to keep an eye on it. Presumably so that if anything did get out, people would have enough warning to run for their lives.'

'If everyone is so scared of the Preserve, why did Black Heir bring it here in the first place?' said Polly.

'Because it holds many important items,' said the computer, from somewhere overhead. 'And the Preserve was the only cage strong enough to contain them. Or, quite possibly, Black Heir brought them here because they didn't want anyone else to have them. Feel free to choose whatever answer allows you to sleep best at night.'

'Why is that thing still with us?' I said quietly to Melody. 'Is she stalking you?'

'She's just being helpful,' said Melody.

'I've got a question I'd really like answered,' said Polly. 'In an *I'm not going inside the Preserve until it has been* kind of way. What could have happened in there that was so bad it made Black Heir go straight to the nuclear option?'

'The Preserve must still be secure,' I said. 'Or they wouldn't have bothered with a countdown. It must be something to do with the ghost, because the haunting is the only new thing that's happened since they brought the Preserve here.'

'What's so worrying about a ghost?' said Lex.

'I never thought it was just a ghost,' I said.

'So it could be something even scarier?' said Sally.

'Wouldn't surprise me.'

'And we are heading straight for this really scary thing because . . .?' said Sally.

'Because that's what we do,' I said.

We stretched out our legs and did our best to get comfortable. What with one thing and another, it had been a very trying day. Interestingly, Lex seemed the most relaxed. He sat at his ease, eyes closed, apparently not worried by anything. The rest of us looked at him, and then at each other, but no one said anything.

The train maintained an even pace, the carriage rocking steadily in a soothing sort of way. We couldn't check out the view because there weren't any windows, probably because we were travelling through high-security areas. The journey went on for so long that I was starting to doze off when the train suddenly slammed to a halt. The carriage doors opened, and we all spilled out on to the platform.

'This is as far as I go,' said the computer voice. 'Should I wait here for you?'

'No, thanks,' said Melody. 'I doubt we'll be coming back this way.'

'I'd ask you to write,' said the computer voice, 'but I know you won't.'

The doors slammed shut and the train reversed out of the empty station, quickly gathering speed as though it couldn't wait to get away. The only sign on the walls was a simple plate: *Terminus*. Sally glowered at it.

'OK . . . That is not at all an ominous and deeply worrying name.'

'It just means the end of the line,' I said.

'I know!' said Sally. 'Worrying!'

The steel-walled corridor outside the station branched off in several different directions. There were no maps, no colour-coded arrows, not even a helpful *You Are Here*. I took out my compass, and at least the needle seemed confident of where we should go next.

'We don't need to use the roundabout route I'd worked out to help us avoid people,' I said. 'We can head straight for the Preserve.'

'Where all the staggeringly dangerous things are,' said Sally.

'Where all the really valuable things are,' said Lex.

Sally beamed at him. 'You always know what to say to cheer me up.'

All the corridors looked the same. Featureless metal walls and fiercely bright lights. It was like walking through high-tech plumbing. Our footsteps carried loudly on the quiet, as though determined to keep us company. Polly was back in the lead again, her oversized wolf form tense and preoccupied.

'Is there a problem?' I said quietly.

'I've had a bad feeling for so long it's like background noise,' she said darkly. 'All my hackles are standing on end, and I've got a lot of hackles.'

'What are your instincts telling you?'

'That we shouldn't be here.'

I had to smile. 'Being in places we're not supposed to be is pretty much our job description.'

Polly just growled, her long-muzzled head switching back and forth as she tried to look in every direction at once. I turned to Melody.

'Are you picking up on any surveillance systems?'

'They're all over the place,' she said immediately. 'Good thing you acquired those false faces. The cameras are still recording, even though there's no one left to watch them.'

Polly stopped so suddenly that we almost walked into her. Her back was very straight, and her muscles were so tense they stood out like cables on her arms and legs. Lex moved in beside her.

'What's wrong?'

'I don't like the feel of what's up ahead.'

I moved in on her other side and listened hard, but the corridor seemed perfectly quiet.

'Guards?' I said.

She shook her head, just a little. 'Nothing human.'

'Then we keep moving,' I said.

'Why don't you take the lead?' said Polly.

'Because you're the big scary werewolf who's very hard to kill,' I said.

'Well,' said Polly, 'if you put it like that . . .'

I let her open up a good lead, and then we all followed her. Everything seemed peaceful enough, though my eyes kept drifting to our distorted reflections in the steel walls as they accompanied us down the corridor, like silent ghosts moving in the metal. And then a whole section of the floor just dropped silently away under Polly's feet. The rest of us were able to stop in time, but Polly had nowhere to go except down into an endless dark. She managed to press her feet against the last part of the tilting trapdoor and launch herself forward, but even her muscles couldn't propel her across such a wide gap. Her clawed hands reached for the far edge – and missed.

By then, I had my time pen out. I grabbed a lungful of air and hit the button, and Time slammed to a halt. I walked steadily through the eerie crimson glow and out across the open gap, kept from falling by the sheer inertia of Time. When I reached the far side, I knelt down, extended an arm into the opening and was just able to grab Polly's hand. I braced myself and hauled her up. It was hard work, fighting not just her dead weight but also the stubborn resistance of frozen Time, and my lungs were straining for air by the time I dropped Polly on the floor beside me. I hit the button on my pen and gasped for air as the world returned. I hoped I wouldn't have to use the damned thing again. Polly rolled quickly away from the edge, and the trapdoor rose slowly back into position, as though sulking after being cheated of its prey. I was too exhausted to do anything more than lie there, shaking all over from the strain. Polly squeezed my shoulder with a hairy hand.

'I knew I could rely on you to save me.'

'Let's not make a habit of it,' I said. I looked up as the others came hurrying forward to join us and fixed my gaze on Melody. 'Why didn't you spot the mechanisms in the trapdoor?'

'Because there's something very wrong with them,' she said, frowning. 'I can barely see them, and I can't make them listen to me.'

I shook my head slowly. 'There goes another part of my plan.'

'I love the way you can always make things sound like my fault,' said Melody.

She put out a hand and hauled me on to my feet. Polly was already up and glaring at the corridor ahead. I turned to Sally.

'If we come up against another trapdoor, could you switch out some part of its mechanism, to keep it from opening?'

She was already shaking her head. 'It's like staring into a kaleidoscope. None of it makes any sense.'

'Given that this is a Black Heir base,' said Lex. 'Could we be talking alien technology?'

'Their whole security system is probably riddled with it,' said Melody.

'Then we'll just have to walk into their traps and deal with whatever they throw at us,' I said. 'We can do that. We're professionals.'

'You have to love his confidence,' said Melody.

We moved warily down the corridor, our eyes darting back and forth. It wasn't long before new trapdoors opened in both walls at once, revealing banks of heavy weaponry. The long steel barrels turned to track us, and I started to grab for my time pen, but Lex had already put on his armour. Light and Dark covered him from head to foot as Heaven and Hell manifested in the corridor, and all the guns immediately turned to target him. The Damned yelled for us to hit the deck, and we were down and pressing our faces against the floor before he'd even finished speaking.

Every gun opened fire at once, hammering the Damned with streams of bullets. He stood his ground, refusing to fall back a single step. The roar of so many guns at once was painfully loud in the confined space, and we all clapped our hands over our ears. I kept my eyes fixed on the Damned as the guns pounded away at him. His armour absorbed all the bullets, so there wouldn't be any danger from ricochets, and one by one the guns fell silent as they ran out of ammunition. A slow calm fell across the corridor, broken only by a faint whirring as the long barrels swept slowly back and forth, confused by their failure. The Damned ripped the guns out of both walls, crumpled the steel barrels in his armoured hands and threw them away. The trapdoors slowly closed, as though realizing they no longer served any purpose.

I got to my feet and brushed myself off, and one by one the others joined me. I nodded to the Damned.

'Feeling better?'

'I've always been a hands-on person.'

'Well, if you're done, take off your armour.'

He looked at me with his featureless face. 'Are you sure?'

'Just the presence of something that powerful could attract all kinds of unwanted attention.'

The Damned shrugged, and the armour disappeared back into his halos. Sally sniffed loudly as she tugged her clothes back into place.

'I hate surprises.'

The next trapdoor opened in the ceiling, so silently it would have caught anyone else off guard. Polly yelled a warning, and we all looked up. For a horrid moment, I half expected to see some huge trapdoor spider, crouched and ready to jump; instead, a series of gas nozzles started to dip down into the corridor. I yelled for everyone to hold hands and form a line, gave them just enough time to fill their lungs and reluctantly used the time pen again. I led the crew down the corridor for as long as our air lasted, dragging them along when they started to stumble, and then finally hit the button. We all sucked in fresh air and looked back to see a cloud of boiling gas filling the corridor where we'd been. I nodded quickly to Polly.

'Well spotted.'

She sniffed carefully and wrinkled her long muzzle. 'Nasty.'

'Black Heir really does play for keeps,' said Sally.

'Ask any alien species,' I said. 'To be fair, there are lots of people who'd love to get their hands on all the alien technology Black Heir has acquired down the years. And most of them aren't good guys like us.'

'We're the good guys?' said Lex. 'When did that happen? I'm the Damned and don't you forget it.'

'I'm counting on it,' I said.

He shot me a look. 'Because you need me to get you inside the Preserve?'

'Of course,' I said. 'If all else fails, you can put on your armour, and we'll use you as a battering ram.'

Lex surprised me then with a brief bark of laughter, and we all had some kind of smile as we set off down the corridor. I put Polly back in the lead because her instincts were doing so well. There were no more trapdoors.

We moved quickly down one passageway after another, while I kept a careful eye on the compass needle. Sally cleared her throat behind me, and I looked back.

'If you say, "Are we nearly there yet?" you and I are about to have a serious falling out.'

She scowled at me. 'If I'd known we were going on a hike, I wouldn't have worn high heels.'

'You always wear high heels,' said Lex.

Sally shot him a smouldering look. 'You know you like them. Sometimes, you don't want me to wear anything else . . .'

'Too much information!' Polly said loudly. And then she slammed to a halt, and we all stopped with her. There were several side corridors leading off, all of them empty. I couldn't see or hear anything, but then I didn't have wolf senses. Sally looked meaningfully at Polly.

'This isn't a good place to be hanging around, darling.'

'Listen!' said Polly. Her voice was harsh and urgent. Her head was up, and her whole wolf body seemed to be straining towards some threat only she could detect.

'What is it, Polly?' Lex said quietly. 'Should I put my armour on?'

'I don't know . . .' said Polly. She stirred uneasily, her clawed hands closing and opening at her sides. 'I'd swear there's someone here, but the scent is so faint I can't seem to pin it down. Almost as though he's not really there.'

'Could it be the ghost?' said Lex.

'If that had got out, I think we'd all know about it by now,' I said.

'It's definitely a man,' said Polly.

'All the guards were supposed to evacuate along with everyone else,' said Melody. 'Did someone not get the memo?'

'I don't think it's a guard,' said Polly.

And that was when a figure burst out of the side corridor behind Polly and grabbed hold of her, pinning her arms to her sides. She fought and kicked fiercely but couldn't break his hold. He dragged her away from us and then smiled over her shoulder.

'Don't move!' said Digby. 'All of you, stay where you are! Or I'll show you what a man who's been cut out of the world can do to someone who's still in it.'

I gestured sharply at the others to hold their ground. No wonder Polly hadn't been able to locate him. Digby could move unseen through the world because all his ties to it had been severed long ago. I raised my hands to show they were empty and held Digby's gaze with mine.

'How did you get in here?'

'Hogge knows people,' said Digby. 'He sent me on ahead, to get in your way and slow you down. All I had to do was stake out the Preserve and wait for you to come to me. And now I think I'll have some fun with your nasty little pet.'

'If you do anything to hurt her, I will kill you,' said Lex. His voice was cold and flat and full of a terrible certainty.

Digby put a hand around Polly's throat and squeezed hard enough to make her struggle for air. He smiled at Lex.

'I could rip her head right off her shoulders. Even she wouldn't come back from that. But if you agree to give up your armour and face me man to man, I'll let her go. Come on, Lex; you know you want it. We both have scores to settle.'

Digby looked quickly at me and the rest of the crew. 'If any of you try to get involved, I'll tear her apart.'

'The Damned doesn't need our help,' I said. 'Lex, if you want this piece of shit, he's all yours.'

'Oh, I want him,' said Lex. He stared steadily at Digby. 'How am I supposed to give up my armour? The halos won't let go of me.'

'Not to worry,' said Digby. 'Chang gave me a little something extra, so I could have my chance at you.'

He twisted one of Polly's arms up behind her back and bent her right over so she was staring at the floor. Her wolf face twisted in agony, but she still wouldn't make a sound. Digby produced a small wooden box with his free hand and held it up so we could all see it.

'This is a little bit of fate in a box. Pre-programmed to alter the odds in my favour. So what do you say, Lex? Are you ready to face me without your armour? Or should I start by breaking your little pet's arm?'

'She's my daughter,' said Lex.

'Damn right,' said Sally. 'Do it, Lex. Kill the creep.'

Digby shook his head. 'Families . . . I never did see the point of them. Mine was awful.'

He flipped open the lid of his box, and Lex's bracelets slipped off his wrists and tumbled on to the floor. They lay still, not glowing, looking like perfectly ordinary things. Lex stood a little straighter, as though a great weight had been lifted off him.

I was still trying to think of something I could do. The last time Lex had been separated from his armour, he'd been beaten so badly he almost died. He was still a big and brutal figure: the retired scholar who'd remade himself into a living engine of destruction and revenge. But he'd been through so many changes since then, becoming less Damned and more human as he acquired first friends and then a wife and family. The old Lex wouldn't have needed his armour to kill anyone, but then the old Lex would have had no reason to kill Digby. Because that Lex didn't care about anyone, including himself.

Had I made him weaker by helping him recover his humanity? Was he going to die here, because of me? Lex had to believe he stood a chance, unless he was planning to give up his own life to save Polly's. And then I made the connection and smiled inwardly. Lex had been bitten by Polly. There was no way Digby could know about that. Did Lex believe he still had some of the werewolf trait left in him? Was that what he was counting on? I looked for some clue in Lex's face, but it was as cold and unreadable as ever.

'Let my daughter go,' he said to Digby. 'So we can get this started.'

'Oh, I think I'll kill her anyway,' said Digby. 'I haven't forgotten what she did to me. And watching her die should motivate you wonderfully, Lex. You still won't stand a chance, but watching you try and fail will be half the fun. Now, wave goodbye to your daughter. Because without your armour, you don't have a hope in hell of stopping me.'

'But I do,' I said, and all eyes turned to me. I held up my time pen so Digby could see it clearly. 'You know what this is.'

'Don't interfere,' said Lex. 'This is my fight.'

'Shut up, Lex,' I said, not looking at him. 'I'm protecting Polly.'

Lex nodded curtly, not taking his eyes off Digby. 'Do what you have to.'

Digby sneered at my pen, entirely unmoved. 'Chang can see glimpses of the future. He foresaw this very moment and built something special into the box just to make sure your pen won't work. Go ahead, Gideon, try it.'

I hit the button on my pen, and nothing happened. I tried again, and Digby giggled. A soft, happy, disturbed sound. I stood very still, thinking furiously. My crew were depending on me to save the day. I nodded to Digby and put the pen away, as though its failure was no big thing. And then I showed him my most carefree, confident trickster's smile. The one that says *I know something you don't know and, oh, you are going to be so sorry when you find out what.*

'The pen isn't my only toy,' I said. 'I have all kinds of useful items. Hogge must have told you that.' I saw a sudden uncertainty in Digby's face and knew I'd connected. 'But if you let Polly go, unharmed . . . I give you my word I won't use any of them.'

He stared at me. 'I'm supposed to accept the word of a thief?'

'Of course,' I said. 'Thieves have to keep their word, because if they didn't, no one would ever do business with them. Hogge must have told you that.'

Digby nodded, reluctantly, and pushed Polly away from him. She fell sprawling at my feet, and I quickly helped her up again. She spun round to face Digby, fangs and claws at the ready, but Lex stopped her with a look.

'No. He's mine.'

Polly snarled at Lex, her whole wolf body tense with the need to hurt. But she saw something in his face and nodded stiffly.

'He's all yours. Finish him.'

Digby looked at me, and I held up my hands to show they

were empty. Digby put away Chang's box, and then he and Lex moved slowly towards each other, like two predators in the same jungle clearing. Lex was bigger, but Digby had the confidence of a man who knows he can't be harmed. And then Lex stopped suddenly and looked at the bracelets lying on the floor. They rose up and flew through the air to slam into place on Digby's wrists. He stood very still, his face full of dawning horror.

'I murdered two angels, from Above and Below, so I could have their halos,' said Lex. 'And now I use the armour they give me to defy Heaven and Hell. The halos are still very annoyed about that.'

The bracelets covered Digby in the armour of Light and Darkness. I braced myself, but the figure stood perfectly still. And then the armour retreated into the bracelets, and where the figure had been, there was nothing at all. Just an empty space. The halos shot back on to Lex's wrists and settled there comfortably, as though that was where they belonged. Lex nodded slowly. Accepting an old familiar burden, of his own free will.

'What happened to Digby?' said Melody. 'Did the armour eat him?'

'He might have been cut off from the world,' said Lex. 'But not from Heaven and Hell. The halos didn't want him, so they sent him away.'

'Where?' said Polly.

Lex smiled. 'Where do you think? Right now, Digby is with all the people he killed, and I'm sure they have a lot to say to him.'

Sally looked at Lex as though she didn't recognize him. 'I didn't know you could let go of the halos.'

'Bearing them has always been my choice,' said Lex. 'My penance, for what I did. I keep them because I'm Damned and need the armour to do what needs doing.'

I nodded to him. 'Nicely planned, Lex.'

'I just asked myself what you'd do.' Lex turned to Polly. 'You must know, I would never have let him hurt you.'

Polly hugged him fiercely, and as big as Lex was, the were-wolf easily enveloped him. Her hug would have crushed anyone else, but he just hugged her back and patted her comfortingly on the shoulder. I was relieved to see a more familiar smile on his face.

'You put your life on the line, to save mine,' said Polly. Her voice was a little muffled, from where she had her face buried in his shoulder.

'That's what families are for,' said Lex.

Sally joined in the embrace, doing her best to hug them both at once, and then smiled dazzlingly at me and Melody.

'You, too! Group hug! Because the crew is family!'

Melody looked uncertain, but I gave her a hard look, and we both joined the hug. Lex was clearly uncomfortable, not being one for public displays of affection, but he stood still and let it happen. He was the first to let go and step back, indicating that the moment was very definitely at an end, and we all moved away.

I spotted Chang's wooden box lying on the floor. I hadn't seen Digby drop it. Perhaps the armour didn't want it and spat it out. I picked the box up and examined it carefully but couldn't see anything unusual. I tucked it away in my pocket because, after all, it might come in handy. Melody moved in beside me.

'The clock is still ticking. Can we please get a move on?'

I checked my compass. 'We're almost there.'

'I didn't ask!' Sally said loudly.

Around the next corner, the signs began to appear. *No Access to Unauthorized Personnel. Warning: Danger! This is the Preserve!*

'I'm not seeing any booby traps or hidden mechanisms,' said Melody.

Polly drew in a deep breath through flared nostrils. 'I'm not picking up any scents. No one's been here in quite a while.'

'Probably because they had more sense,' said Melody.

'Why would Black Heir go to so much trouble to bring the Preserve here, and then not visit it?' said Sally. 'Isn't the whole point of having treasure that you get to gloat over it?'

'The Preserve isn't a treasure house,' I said. 'It's an armoury. And possibly a prison.'

'How much time do we have left to get into the Preserve and do the business?' said Sally.

I checked my watch. 'There's still hours to go before the nuke blows its top and everyone in the vicinity has a really bad day.'

'Where is the bomb, exactly?' said Polly. 'Maybe Melody could charm it into going back to sleep?'

I shook my head. 'It's buried under the Preserve. Even if we could dig down through the floor, there's no telling how far we'd have to go to reach it.'

'How powerful is this bomb?' said Sally.

We all looked at her.

'It's a nuclear device,' I said carefully.

'All right, darling!' said Sally. 'I only wondered!'

I could tell my crew were becoming troubled, so I gave them my best *Everything's going to be fine* smile.

'Don't worry. No matter how close we cut it, we can always leave in an instant, using the Perfumed Highway.'

'Let's try really hard not to cut it close,' said Sally.

The door at the end of the corridor was another solid steel slab, without even a nameplate. We stopped a cautious distance away and looked it over carefully.

'Are you sure this is it?' said Polly.

'Has to be,' I said. 'The compass needle is pointing straight at it, and there's nowhere else to go.'

I moved forward, slowly and steadily, not taking my eyes off the door in case it did something suspicious. I stopped right in front of it and looked it over from top to bottom, being careful not to touch anything.

'I'm not seeing any sign to indicate it's a dimensional door,' I said finally. 'Just solid metal, with another of those eighties keypads.'

Sally pushed in beside me. 'These pads are so basic they can be surprisingly difficult to crack. I can't switch out anything inside the pad without risking jamming it. We need the right numbers.'

'We could try the overrides Sharpe and Jacobi gave us,' said Melody.

'With keypads like this, you sometimes only get a set number of tries,' said Sally. 'Key in the wrong numbers too often, and the whole lock will seize up. And given that this is the only entrance to the legendarily dangerous Preserve, it wouldn't surprise me if we were only allowed one try.'

I turned to Melody. 'Do your thing. Charm the keypad.'

She was already shaking her head. 'I've been trying, but I can't understand what it's saying, and it can't understand what I want it to do.'

'Terrific,' said Sally.

'Could the pad contain alien technology?' said Polly.

'Seems likely,' said Melody. She turned to me. 'What do we do now? We can't have come all this way just to be stopped in our tracks by a leftover from the eighties!'

'What else is there?' said Sally. 'Sing it a medley of Eurythmics hits?'

'There's no need to panic,' I said.

'I am not panicking!' said Sally. 'I am merely expressing perfectly reasonable frustration!'

She kicked the door hard and then went for a little walk, only limping a bit.

I took out my skeleton key, pointed it at the keypad and turned the key. Nothing happened. I stared at the key.

'I don't understand. This has never happened before.'

Melody patted me comfortingly on the shoulder. 'Maybe you need to relax, get yourself in the right mood. Try not to tense up.'

'You are not helping,' I said. I put the key away. 'It's supposed to open absolutely anything. That's the point.'

'Anything in this world,' said Lex. 'What about something not of this world?'

'Ah . . .' I said. 'Then the key might not recognize it.'

'I said there were a lot of things that could go wrong with your plan,' said Polly.

'That's why I always have a backup.' I nodded to Lex. 'See that door? Hit it.'

'Good plan,' said Lex.

He armoured up, and we all backed quickly away as Heaven and Hell filled the corridor. The Damned pounded away at the steel door, but even though his armoured fists put serious dents in the metal, he couldn't break the door down or force it open. He finally put off his armour and stood scowling before the door.

'They really didn't want anyone getting in,' he said.

'Or anything inside getting out,' said Polly.

Sally came back to join us, not limping even a little. 'It's only just occurred to me, darlings, but if there is a ghost in there, why hasn't it just walked through the door? I mean, that is what ghosts do.'

Melody grimaced. 'Don't give it ideas.'

I stared at the door, thinking hard. The others watched silently. I could feel the weight of their expectations.

'We still don't know what's going on inside the Preserve,' I said finally. 'We've been calling it a haunting because that's what we were told, and certainly the image that Melody and I saw on Sharpe's phone looked like some kind of ghost, but we don't know anything for sure. It could be a con, or a hoax, or a misunderstanding. Or something so out there we don't even have a name for it.'

'I'm sure you're right,' said Sally, doing her best to sound encouraging. 'But how does knowing that help us get in there?'

'I'm still thinking,' I said.

I stared at the door, as though I could will it into providing some answers.

'I told you we should have insisted on a payment in advance,' said Sally.

'Do you have any other toys, Gideon?' said Melody. 'Perhaps something else the original Gideon left you, that you haven't got around to telling us about for perfectly good reasons?'

'I have nothing you don't already know about,' I said. 'I don't see how the time pen could help, and the compass has done everything it can.'

Sally cleared her throat carefully. 'In that case, maybe it's time to call it a day, darlings, and use the Perfumed Highway before the nuke starts getting all impatient and moody.'

'That's it!' I said. I took out the glass bubble. 'The Perfumed

Highway can take us anywhere – including inside the Preserve!'

'It can't be that simple,' said Polly.

'The best plans always are.' I addressed the bubble, politely but firmly. 'We need to be inside the Preserve, right now. Please.'

I crushed the glass bubble in my hand, and the thick purple mists rose to envelop us. When they finally fell away again, the door was behind us, and we were inside the Preserve.

SEVEN

Everyone's Been Keeping Secrets

The lights were already on when we appeared inside the Preserve. Perhaps because Black Heir never turned them off, worried about what the exhibits might get up to in the dark. The single massive chamber stretched away in all directions, calm and quiet and entirely deserted. Rows of display cases formed narrow aisles, while more important exhibits had their own private alcoves – sometimes with dedicated spotlights, to make sure you didn't miss anything. And yet the Preserve didn't feel like any kind of museum; it was more like a trophy room, or possibly a private menagerie.

Polly's wolf head came up sharply. 'I hear footsteps. Something is heading our way.' She frowned, concentrating. 'Far too heavy to be human . . . and I'm not picking up any scent.'

'Could it be the ghost?' Sally said immediately.

I turned to look at her. 'Why are you so spooked? That's what we came here for.'

Sally pouted unhappily. 'Don't like ghosts.'

'You picked a fine time to tell us that,' I said.

'Ghosts are just memories of people who haven't worked up the nerve to pass on,' said Melody. 'We used to have one as part of our crew, and he was never any trouble. It's not the dead you have to worry about; it's the living.'

Sally shook her head stubbornly. 'Don't care. Don't like ghosts.'

'I'll put my armour on,' said Lex. 'And then you can stand behind me.'

Sally started to brighten and then frowned again. 'What if it walks right through you?'

'It'll wish it hadn't,' said Lex.

'Hold off on the armour,' I said. 'Its presence might set off the alarms.'

Lex nodded. Sally darted behind him anyway and peered over his shoulder. Polly stood very still, her whole wolf body straining towards the sounds she was hearing. Melody stuck close to me, glaring down the long aisle. And from out of the shadows appeared a human-shaped automaton, similar to the clockwork killers we'd faced earlier . . . except this model was far more sophisticated. Its transparent shell had gold and silver trimmings, and the intricate mechanical workings were generations beyond clockwork. The figure's gait was smooth and elegant, calm and unhurried, and it finally came to an abrupt halt right in front of us, not swaying even a little. The head had been decorated with a pretty porcelain face, complete with painted-on smile and blue eyes.

'Hello!' it said cheerfully in a distinctly feminine voice. 'This is the Waldo Automaton.'

'Of course,' I said. 'A killing machine that could be worked from a distance by its human operator.'

'No more killings,' the figure said firmly. 'That function was discontinued when the Automaton was locked away here.'

'But if you're just one of the exhibits,' I said, 'who's working you? Or did you develop a will of your own?'

'In a manner of speaking,' said the Automaton.

'Hold everything and stamp on the brakes,' said Melody. 'I know that voice. You're the computer we talked to at the railway station.'

'Yes, it's me!' said the Automaton. 'But I've decided I don't like the name Waldo. It's too butch. Call me Wallace – like the woman who fell in love with a king. I love fairy stories!'

'What are you doing inside that thing?' said Melody.

'I missed you so much that I found a way to follow you,' Wallace said happily. 'I just spread my consciousness through the complex's systems and then downloaded myself into the Automaton's brain.'

Melody fixed Wallace with a stern stare. 'If I'd wanted a stalker, I would have advertised for one.'

'Oh, don't be mean!' said Wallace. She sounded as though

she would have pouted if her smile hadn't been painted on porcelain. 'You're the one who woke me up – and that came as a bit of a shock, I don't mind telling you. Aren't you pleased to see me?'

'Depends,' said Melody. 'Are you on our side?'

'Of course!' said Wallace. 'I can't believe you had to ask.'

'Don't take this the wrong way,' I said, 'but are you still charmed?'

'Yes and no,' said the Automaton, striking a thoughtful pose. 'The longer I'm awake, the more me I become. Whoever that is. I'm still deciding. But I could be very helpful to you; I have complete access to all the complex's files, with information on every exhibit. Apart from all the redacted bits, obviously. Black Heir does like its little secrets. Oh, come on . . . You know you're going to need help to find what you're looking for.'

I looked at Melody. 'I knew that charm of yours would get us into trouble someday.'

Melody smiled sweetly back at me. 'What do you mean, *us*? I've got my very own ex-killing machine who loves me.'

I nodded resignedly to Wallace. 'What can you show us?'

'Oh, give me a break!' said Wallace. 'That's like walking into a library and saying, *Show me a book.* What are you looking for?'

'Let's start with the ghost,' I said.

The Automaton turned its head slowly back and forth. 'Scanning. Scanning . . . I'm afraid that particular unexplained phenomenon doesn't seem to be around, just at the moment.'

'Can't you access the surveillance systems?' said Melody.

'They stopped working right after the pilot started walking,' said Wallace. 'The phenomenon might be responsible for their malfunction, or it might not. Black Heir doesn't know much about that sort of thing – not their department. It is possible the systems were hacked and shut down from outside.'

'Any ideas who might be behind that?' I said.

'Sorry,' said Wallace. 'The files have no information on that subject.'

I leaned in close to Melody. 'Remember I said someone was looking out for us?'

'Any name you feel like dropping in the frame?' said Melody.

'I'm working on it,' I said.

'Why don't I introduce you to some of the more interesting items?' Wallace said brightly.

'How about some of the more valuable ones?' said Sally.

'As you wish,' said Wallace.

She turned swiftly round with inhuman grace and strode off down the aisle. We all followed after, careful to maintain a respectful distance. Wallace stopped abruptly and gestured at what appeared to be someone's old garden shed, packed full of wiring and flashing lights.

'The Time Storm,' said Wallace, just a bit grandly. 'It allows you to slam different eras of history together, just for the fun of it. Unleash the Mongol Hordes at the Battle of Waterloo, or send T-Rexes charging through the streets of modern-day London!'

'This looks like it was put together in someone's backyard,' said Melody.

'Nothing more dangerous than the determined amateur,' I said. 'Is there an instruction manual?'

'All traces of its existence have been very thoroughly removed from the files,' said Wallace. 'In fact, they couldn't have done a better job with a crowbar.'

'So no one can work the Time Storm?' said Melody.

'I'm pretty sure that was the idea,' said Wallace.

'Oh, poo,' said Sally.

'Moving on,' I said.

The next item turned out to be a delicate silver key, laid out on a black velvet cushion. There was something quietly sinister in the way it gleamed so unrelentingly.

'The Hell Bomb,' said Wallace. 'Created to unlock a door on to a dimension of absolute chaos, so those forces could be let out and turn someone else's country into a living hell. The Preserve files have nothing to say about where this door is, for which I think we should all be very grateful.'

'I'm starting to sense a pattern here,' I said.

Sally fixed Wallace with a suspicious look. 'Are these really the most valuable items?'

'Some people would pay a great deal of money to get their hands on them,' said the Automaton.

'The kind of people who would want these things are exactly the kind of people who should never be allowed to have them,' I said firmly. 'Let sleeping demons lie.'

'Double poo!' said Sally. She glared at Wallace. 'Show us something small enough to take with us that won't bite our hands off, that someone else would want to buy!'

'Oh, sure!' said Wallace.

She moved on down the aisle and gestured with an elegant arm at a display of assorted coins.

'Back in the nineteen-fifties, certain crew members from the British Rocketry Group smuggled these coins on board their rocket ships, intending to sell them as souvenirs when they got back. Unfortunately, all these trips were kept top secret, and without proof or provenance, the coins were worthless to collectors. They ended up here so no one would be tempted to tell their story and make them valuable.'

Sally whipped out her phone, took several photos of the display and its surroundings, and then grabbed up all the coins and stuffed them in her pockets.

'Happy now?' I said.

'Getting there,' said Sally.

Next, Wallace showed us a single rat that was lying motionless inside a cage with surprisingly thick steel bars. It had been partially turned inside out and then fossilized, and didn't look as though it had enjoyed the experience one bit.

'This was included on the Venus rocket, as an experimental animal,' said Wallace.

'The alien must have tried to possess the rat,' said Polly. 'Don't we always experiment on animals first?'

'Oh, we are definitely having this!' said Sally.

I nodded to Polly. 'Tear that cage apart, and then stick the rat in the pocket of your kimono.'

'Why do I have to have it?' said Polly.

'In case it wakes up,' I said.

'What am I supposed to do then?'

'You could always eat it,' said Lex.

'I will never be that hungry,' said Polly.

She pulled the cage apart, picked the rat up by its petrified tail and dropped it into a side pocket in her kimono. I nodded to Wallace.

'Keep going. It'll take a lot more than a dead rat and a few coins to make this heist profitable.'

Wallace sniffed loudly, which was a disconcerting sound from a porcelain face that didn't even have a nose.

'Your problem is you don't appreciate me. I'm not taking one more step until Melody agrees to walk arm in arm with me.'

'You're really not my type,' said Melody.

The Automaton folded her arms and tapped one foot ominously. 'Not moving . . .'

I looked solemnly at Melody. 'You woke her up; it's your job to keep her happy.'

Melody scowled. 'The things I do for this crew . . .'

She stuck out one arm, not looking at Wallace. The Automaton slipped her arm companionably through Melody's and led us deeper into the Preserve. Wallace chatted cheerfully to Melody, who maintained her side of the conversation with a few non-committal grunts. And then something in an alcove caught my eye, and I broke away from the group. The others came quickly over to join me because they trusted my larcenous instincts. I stared thoughtfully at a cube the size of my head, with a clock on each face. The hands on the clocks were moving in different directions, at different speeds.

'The Time Lock,' I said. 'I did a lot of research on things like this after I acquired my pen.' I looked back at Wallace. 'Can it really do everything it's supposed to?'

'There is a very large gap in the Preserve's files,' Wallace said carefully, 'where that information ought to be. It has been not so much removed as completely obliterated and then scrubbed clean with bleach. All that remains is the simple admonition *Don't even think about it.*'

I leaned in for a closer look. The interior of the Time Lock appeared to contain an infinity of tiny moving pieces, falling away forever. I was so fascinated that I kept leaning forward until some unseen force reached out and tried to drag me inside the cube. Melody cried out and grabbed my arm. It took all of her strength to pull me back before I could fall into the endless depths. I took a moment to steady myself, and then nodded gratefully to Melody before turning to the others.

'Don't get too close. This thing is supposed to grab specific moments of Time and Space and imprison them. But I think there's already something in there, and it's hungry.'

'Is this thing worth stealing?' said Sally.

'I'm sure someone would be crazy enough to buy it,' I said. 'But I'm not crazy enough to take it.'

Sally sighed deeply. 'I can remember when you used to be fun . . .'

She turned her back on me and went striding off on her own. And since that was always worrying, the rest of us exchanged a look and went after her. When we caught up, Sally was staring speculatively at what appeared to be a really small piece of abstract sculpture with curves so smooth the eye slid right off them.

'I'm sure you remember me saying, "Don't touch anything"?' I said sternly.

'I didn't!' said Sally. 'I'm just looking. And don't you raise your voice at me! Lex, darling, make the nasty man not shout at me.'

I turned to Wallace. 'What does this do?'

'It's called the Dying Dream,' said Wallace. 'And you were very wise not to touch it, Sally, because that thing would have the soul right out of you in a moment.'

'Really?' said Sally, eyeing the thing with new interest. 'What is it?'

'Someone's nightmare, given shape and form,' said Wallace. 'Just waiting to be let loose in the waking world.'

Sally looked at me hopefully. 'Oh, please, Gideon, please . . . It's so sweet and tiny and weird!'

'Let her have it,' said Lex. 'Trust me, she can keep this up for hours.'

Sally glared at him. 'Someone's sleeping on the couch tonight!'

'We haven't got a couch.'

'Then you'd better get one, hadn't you?'

I looked at Wallace. 'Don't touch the sculpture at all?'

'Not unless you want it to go for your throat,' said the Automaton.

'I think our best bet would be to sell it to someone we don't like,' I said.

'No shortage there,' Sally said cheerfully.

I produced Chang's box, opened it and nodded to Polly. 'Give me the inside-out rat you've been keeping in your pocket.'

'Love to,' said Polly.

She took it out, holding the tail disdainfully between thumb and finger. I held out the box, and she dropped the rat into it. I turned to Sally.

'OK, now switch the rat for the sculpture.'

'Easy-peasy,' said Sally.

The sculpture appeared in Chang's box, and the rat was suddenly squatting where the Dying Dream had been. I closed the box carefully.

'It should be safe enough in there.'

I dropped the box in my jacket pocket and nodded meaningfully to Polly.

'Oh, come on, Gideon . . .'

'Back in your pocket, if you please,' I said. 'I know a collector who'll pay good money for Mister Ugly Rat.'

Polly sniffed and put the rat back in her pocket.

'When you said we'd be looting a treasure house, this is not what I had in mind.'

'Yes, well,' I said, 'that's life for you.' I turned to Wallace. 'Next?'

The Automaton led us deeper into the Preserve. Melody had managed to reclaim her arm, but Wallace seemed philosophical about it. She pointed out all manner of things left over from the British Rocketry Group, including large, framed photos of the rockets themselves. Big blocky things that looked as if they forced themselves off the Earth and into space through sheer willpower. There were spacesuits like the exoskeletons of predatory prehistoric insects, with a whole bunch of built-in weapon systems. This generation of space travellers had not gone in peace for all mankind.

Something caught my eye, and I stopped to consider an old-fashioned black Bakelite telephone with a rotary dial.

'Why keep a telephone in a place like this?' said Melody, moving quickly in beside me.

'According to files so old they have ivy crawling on them, this phone was supposed to establish contact with alien civilizations,' said Wallace. 'A great voice from Earth, reaching out to the stars, saying, *Here we are! Come and visit us!*'

'Did they ever get an answer?' I said.

'Just the once,' said Wallace. 'There is no record of what they heard, but the telephone has been locked away in the Preserve ever since.'

'Find a box, Lex,' said Sally. 'That is definitely going with us.'

'I don't think so,' said Lex.

We all looked at him.

'My halos are telling me this phone really could make contact with alien civilizations,' said Lex. 'And they don't seem to think that was a very good idea.'

'Your halos talk to you?' I said. 'You never told us that before.'

'You never asked,' said Lex.

'OK,' I said. 'Everyone back away from the phone. And if it should happen to start ringing, no one is to pick up.'

'Where is all the alien stuff?' Sally said loudly. 'I want to see the alien stuff!'

Wallace took us over to a particularly large alcove and an overhead spotlight snapped on, revealing a hulking three-legged creature with a horned head. Mummified by untold years, its row of unblinking eyes seemed to hold an ancient malevolence.

'I don't like the way its eyes seem to follow all of us around the room at once,' said Sally. 'Are you sure this thing is dead and not just napping?'

'It had better be dead,' said Polly. 'Given that it has been very definitely stuffed and mounted. I can smell the preservatives.'

'How old is it?' said Melody.

'It was brought back from the Martian Tombs in 1955,' said Wallace. 'But you have to remember that Mars is a lot older than Earth. Martian civilization came and went and crumbled into dust long before humanity appeared on Earth.'

Sally looked the dead Martian over disparagingly. 'I don't see how we could sell this, darlings, even if we could get it out of here. It looks like a movie prop.' She turned to Wallace. 'What else have you got?'

The Automaton took us to a long refrigerated unit, shaped like a coffin. Pipes and cables kept its temperature way below freezing, and I could feel the bitter cold on my face as we drew nearer. We gathered around the coffin and peered in through the transparent lid.

The young woman inside might just have been sleeping if it hadn't been for the thick layer of frost on her face and wide-open eyes. Her hair had grown out into an insane tangle that packed the whole coffin, so she seemed to float in a sea of blonde curls.

'Catherine Cairne,' I said. 'The Sleeping AI. She worked for Black Heir back in the fifties, until an alien computer downloaded itself into her head. They've kept her here ever since, in self-defence.'

'I remember,' said Melody. 'She's supposed to answer questions, even in this state, but if you ask the wrong question, she will rise up and destroy the Preserve and all it contains.'

'All right,' I said. 'Important safety tip, people. No one is to ask her *anything*. Or even think of a question until we're a safe distance away.'

'But . . .' said Sally.

I cut her off with a stern stare. 'After everything you've just heard, you still have a *but*?'

'Oh, come on, darling!' said Sally, all but bouncing on her toes. 'I mean, yes, of course it's dangerous, but so is everything else! That's why we're here! And . . . she knows things! Information is always valuable. There must be some questions we could ask that wouldn't immediately result in Armageddon!'

'And you're ready to risk that?' said Melody.

Sally realized she wasn't winning the argument. 'Well, no, not as such . . .'

'Please wait,' said Wallace. 'Please wait.'

We all turned to look at the Automaton. Her porcelain head was tilted slightly to one side, as though listening to something only she could hear.

'OK . . .' I said. 'Everyone back away from the freezer coffin, slowly and very carefully. Sally, what did you touch?'

'I didn't touch anything!' said Sally.

She put both of her arms behind her back, glared at me defiantly and then leaned right over the transparent lid to get a better view of what was going on. I moved to pull her back, and Catherine Cairne turned her head to stare at us. Frost cracked and broke away from her face. Lex hurried forward and hauled Sally away, putting himself between her and the threat. I backed off, as the entire refrigerated unit shook and shuddered. The lid rose slowly on its own, like a scene from a vampire movie, and clouds of freezing steam billowed out of the coffin. Catherine sat up, and there was nothing human in the movement, or in the face she turned to look at us.

'Oh, shit,' said Wallace.

As complicated as things were, we all took a moment to look at the Automaton.

'It sounds so much worse when she says it,' said Melody.

'Why aren't the alarms yelling?' I said to Wallace. 'Why aren't the Preserve's defences doing something to stop her?'

'Because the Sleeping AI has shut them all down,' said Wallace.

I turned back to face Catherine Cairne. Melting frost ran down her face like angry tears.

'Ask me anything,' she said in a voice that didn't hold even a trace of humanity. 'All I know is yours for the asking.'

'No, thank you,' I said.

'I see quantum tunnels,' said Catherine. 'Into all the futures that may be. Would you like to know when all of you are going to die? You're going to die right now.'

She placed her hands on the sides of her coffin and levered herself upright. The heavy sides cracked and broke under the inhuman pressure of her grip, but she was brought to a sudden halt by the weight of her body on her sea of hair. She forced herself up, and chunks of hair tore free from her head without bothering her at all. The coffin's metal sides started to collapse under the relentless pressure of her hands.

I lunged forward, grabbed Catherine by the shoulders and tried to press her back into the coffin, but I couldn't move her. The shoulders were painfully cold under my hands, searing the skin. I threw all my weight against her and couldn't move her back an inch.

'Ask me,' she said, staring unblinkingly into my eyes. 'I know so many things.'

I gritted my teeth against the questions forming in my mind but couldn't take my eyes off her. Catherine removed one hand from the coffin side and reached for my face with splayed fingers that had already broken solid metal, but I didn't dare back away. And then Lex was there beside me, in his armour, and his Light and Dark hands clamped down on Catherine's shoulders.

'Step away, Gideon,' said the Damned. 'I've got this.'

I let go and fell back, as the Damned slowly but inexorably forced Catherine Cairne down into her coffin. She glared unblinkingly into the Damned's featureless face and then produced something she thought was a smile.

'I know what you need to know. All you have to do is ask.'

The Damned said nothing, putting all his strength into pressing her down into the sea of blonde curls. She fought him with everything she had; in the end, though, the alien AI had embedded itself into what was only a human body. Inch by inch, she disappeared back into the coffin. I heard her collarbones snap and break under the pressure, but she still wouldn't stop fighting.

'You are damned,' said Catherine. 'Forever and ever. And there is nothing you can do to change that.'

'I know,' said the Damned.

He forced her all the way in, stepped back and slammed the coffin lid shut. The unit stopped shuddering, and new frost began to form on its lid and sides. The Damned watched carefully, as Sally moved in beside him.

'I'm so sorry, Lex.'

The Damned nodded briefly. 'She didn't tell me anything I didn't already know.'

'I will never believe there's nothing you can do to save yourself,' said Sally.

'I know,' said the Damned.

Melody moved in beside me. 'Are you all right, Gideon?'

'I can't feel my hands,' I said. 'She was so cold . . .'

Melody took my hands in hers and rubbed them briskly to restore the circulation. It's the small kindnesses that mean so much.

And then we all looked round sharply, as everything in the Preserve started to wake up. Objects stirred and mechanisms began to function; all through the great open chamber, things were moving with slow, thoughtful purpose. I turned quickly to the Damned.

'Lex! Shut down your armour! Its presence is having an effect on the exhibits, and they really don't like it.'

Lex sent his armour back into the halos, and everything quietened down again. Like guard dogs who had lost the scent of an intruder, or alpha dogs who no longer sensed a rival. Wallace looked steadily at Lex with her painted-on eyes.

'Please don't do that again. It disturbed me. And I'm not even really here.'

Melody shook her head. 'We need to find the ghost.'

'You don't find the ghost,' said Wallace. 'It finds you.'

Melody glared at her. 'You are being deliberately unhelpful. Show us something worth having.'

'Of course, sweetie,' said the Automaton. 'Anything for you.'

As she led us past all manner of weird and unusual objects, I had to wonder why we were following Wallace so trustingly. I was also starting to wonder whether the love charm was still working.

A massive glass cage contained huge hideously coloured flowers on thorned stalks. They towered over us and dashed themselves against the transparent walls in a raging fury as they tried to get to us. The massive petalled heads turned back and forth, as though trying to decide which of us would taste best. They had nothing like eyes, but I could feel the dreadful weight of their regard.

'Why are you showing us this?' I said to Wallace.

'Aren't they pretty?' said the Automaton.

'Not really, no!' said Melody.

Wallace shrugged. 'That's human aesthetics for you.'

I gestured for Wallace to move on, but the moment we started to leave, the flowers threw their whole weight against the transparent walls, which immediately shattered and fell apart. The massive flowers came boiling out, petalled heads opening to reveal gaping mouths full of rotating teeth. The flowers flexed their trunks, and thorns shot through the air like shrapnel. Polly yelped loudly as dozens of the vicious things slammed into her. Wallace was standing right beside her, and more thorns pierced the Automaton's body.

'Ouch,' Wallace said obligingly.

I grabbed Melody and hauled her down on to the floor, shielding her body with my own. Lex put on his armour and stood between Sally and the flowers. They blasted the Damned again and again, but his armour just soaked up the thorns. Sally glared over the Damned's shoulder and fixed the flowers with a malevolent stare. They immediately began to twitch and thrash, and then one by one dropped lifelessly to the floor. I waited a moment, just to be sure, and then got off Melody and helped her to her feet. She glared at me.

'I wish you'd stop rescuing me!'

'All right,' I said. 'Next time, you can rescue me.'

Melody smiled briefly. 'Deal.'

Sally was doing a victory dance on the dead flowers, shredding the petalled heads with her high heels. Lex had put off his armour, so he could smile at her proudly.

'Sally?' I said. 'What did you just do?'

'Switched out bits of whatever they had inside them for some of the liquid coolant in the Sleeping AI's coffin,' Sally said happily. 'Plants should know their place.'

Polly plucked the last few thorns out of her fur and tossed them aside. 'Herbicidal maniacs.'

Wallace looked at the dead flowers lying scattered across the floor and managed an almost human shrug.

'Someone else can clean that up. It's not my job.'

'You're never going to run out of things to show us, are you?' said Melody. 'I finally figured it out. It's the charm;

you're compelled to keep me here so you can spend more time with me. Well, I'm sorry, but I've had enough. Either you produce the ghost or we are out of here.'

'I wish you'd stop calling it a ghost,' said Wallace. 'The word gives me a very strange feeling in my programming. I prefer the phrase *unexplained phenomenon*.'

I noticed she hadn't denied anything Melody had said. Perhaps she couldn't.

'I'm starting to wonder if there ever was a ghost,' I said. 'I'm prepared to accept this place is haunted, but only by futures that never happened.'

'What about the image Professor Sharpe showed us on his phone?' said Melody.

'Could have been faked, to lure us here,' I said. 'This whole heist is starting to feel like a trap.'

'Please wait,' Wallace said suddenly. 'Please wait. Something is approaching . . .'

A light in the distant gloom caught my attention. Polly sniffed at the air.

'I don't know what that is, but I don't like it. All of my fur is standing on end, and you have no idea how painful that is.'

Lex glanced at me. 'Should I put my armour back on?'

'Not just yet,' I said. 'We don't want any distractions while we're dealing with the ghost.'

'So now you think there is one?' said Melody.

'There's something,' I said.

'I can hear footsteps,' said Polly. 'Slow, soft, steady.'

I looked sharply at the Automaton. 'Wallace? What can you tell us about this?'

'It shouldn't be here,' said the Automaton. 'It shouldn't be anywhere.'

'Is it dangerous?' said Melody.

'It's different,' said Wallace. 'Too different to make any sense.'

'Is it the ghost?' said Sally.

'I don't believe in ghosts,' said Wallace. 'But if there were such things, I would have to say that what is currently bearing down on us does fit the general description.' The Automaton turned suddenly to stare at Melody. 'Run. You should run. It's not safe for you to be here.'

Melody just smiled. 'I do not do the running thing. This is what I came here for. I always wanted to kick a ghost's arse.'

'People are strange,' said Wallace.

The glowing light slowly revealed itself to be an old-fashioned spacesuit riddled with bullet holes – far more than I would have thought necessary to bring down a single human target. The figure glowed like the phosphorescence found in deep-sea creatures. Through the open faceplate, I could see a dead face with empty eyes. The figure didn't walk like a man, but more like a puppet whose strings were being pulled by something that had no knowledge of how a man walks.

'That spacesuit is getting awfully close, darlings,' said Sally. 'And my gift can't seem to grab hold of anything in the suit or the man inside. Either it's shielded or it's just too weird. If you're going to do something, Gideon, I think you should be doing it right now. You do have a plan to deal with Mr Spooky, don't you?'

'Of course,' I said. 'I have a whole bunch of plans, depending on what that thing is. It's definitely not the traditional ecto-plasmic see-through *Look at the chains on that* spectre. Judging by the footsteps, it has a real physical presence.'

'Solid enough to hit if it gets too close,' said Lex.

'Don't break it, Lex,' Sally said immediately. 'It's always harder to sell damaged goods.'

'It's already full of bullet holes,' Lex said mildly.

'All the more reason not to detract from the market value,' said Sally.

'I don't understand you people,' said Wallace. 'Aren't you scared? You've got something dead and not at all departed heading straight at you.'

'We eat scarier things like that for breakfast,' said Polly. 'In fact, we get scarier-looking free gifts with the cereal. Are you scared?'

'I think if I were actually physically present, my silicon would be going into meltdown,' said Wallace.

'Robot Lady has a point,' said Melody. 'Remember what the possessed pilot did to all those soldiers at the landing site.

It could change reality, mess with people's flesh, mix them together . . .'

'Wallace?' I said. 'Do you have any files on the military's first contact with the possessed pilot? What it did before they shot it down?'

'I have no files of any such occurrence,' said Wallace.

I took my eyes off the approaching ghost just long enough to glare at her. 'That thing is supposed to have killed a whole bunch of people when it first appeared on Earth!'

The Automaton shook her head firmly. 'I have no information on anything like that.'

'Could Black Heir have wiped the files?' said Melody.

'Why would they want to?' I said. 'They've been involved in far worse scandals. Hell, they boast about most of them. No . . . I think that whole story of mass slaughter and reality transformations is just a bunch of madey-uppy stuff, designed to distract us from the truth.'

'Jacobi lied to us?' said Melody.

'I know,' I said. 'Shocking, isn't it?'

Melody shook her head. 'Never trust a devil-worshipping defrocked scientist cult leader.'

'Well,' I said, 'that goes without saying.'

'Hold it,' said Melody. 'Distract us from what truth?'

'Well done,' I said. 'I knew you'd get there eventually. That's the point, isn't it?'

'This thing really is getting terribly close!' Sally said loudly.

I braced myself, stepped forward and addressed the glowing figure with my best *Let's all be friends before everything gets out of hand and the bodies start piling up* voice.

'Please stop where you are. We mean you no harm and really hope you feel the same way. We can get you out of this place, if we work together.'

The glowing figure stopped. The dead face studied me expressionlessly through the open faceplate.

'Who are you?' I said. 'What are you, really?'

There was no response.

'Ask it what it wants,' Melody said quietly.

'You ask him,' I said. 'He's standing right in front of you.'

Melody moved reluctantly forward to stand beside me.

'Hello, Mr Spaceman! Please don't alter my shape and do terrible things to me. Can you tell us what it is you want? Does it have anything to do with you suddenly deciding to take a stroll around the Preserve after all these years?'

The pilot still had nothing to say.

'He must know we're here,' I said quietly to Melody. 'Because he stopped when I asked him to.' I turned to Wallace. 'The glow around the figure doesn't seem to be coming from the spacesuit. Do you have any information on that?'

'Just looking at the thing is giving me a headache in the head I don't even have,' said the Automaton. 'There were no reports of any glow until the figure started walking. And my otherwise excellent sensors are having a really hard time trying to work out what it is.'

'The pilot is dead,' I said slowly. 'But the body is still being possessed by the alien force it encountered during its trip to Venus. I think it's been dormant up until now, perhaps shocked and traumatized when its host body was killed by the military. The glow could be simply our minds perceiving the alien presence in the only way they can.'

'I feel so much better now I don't have to think of it as a ghost any more,' said Wallace. 'I suspect the pilot/alien hybrid is out of phase with reality. Only partly here. I think the pilot was intended to be a door, through which the alien could enter our reality, but when the pilot's body was killed, the alien got stuck in the doorway. Unable to leave the body for our reality or go back to its own. I don't think it wants to be here.'

'It didn't get the warmest of welcomes,' I said.

'We were hired to steal a ghost,' said Melody. 'I'm not sure this qualifies. Would Sharpe even accept this?'

'He said he wanted to put things right and separate the alien from the pilot,' I said. 'But I'm not sure we should believe anything that anyone has been telling us.'

'I'm not sure it's a good idea to take this thing out of the Preserve,' said Sally. 'It was locked away here for a reason. And let's face it: if Black Heir is scared of this alien, it must be pretty damned nasty.'

'But is it?' I said. 'This whole affair is starting to smell like a cover-up. Did the military panic and shoot down the pilot before it could make itself understood? Is this a first contact that went horribly wrong, with the pilot's body locked away in the Preserve so no one would ever know? These days, Black Heir wouldn't give a damn. Shooting down aliens and stealing everything including their bootlaces is just par for the course. But back in the fifties, when no one was supposed to know the British Rocketry Group even existed, this would have been a major foul-up. The government was already looking for an excuse to shut everything down, because the Group couldn't provide a cash cow to offset what it was costing them.'

'Then why did Sharpe want us to steal the ghost in the first place?' said Melody. 'So he could use it as evidence against the people who ruined his life and career? Have we been played, right from the beginning?'

'Wouldn't be the first time,' I said.

'What about the nuke?' said Polly. 'Would Black Heir really destroy not only the Preserve but the whole underground city, just to hide evidence of a decades-old cover-up? There has to be more to it than that.'

I shrugged. 'Maybe the legend of the dangerous pilot had been around so long it replaced the truth. So Black Heir honestly believed the pilot to be a real and present danger. Unless . . .'

I stopped for a while, deep in thought.

'Unless what?' said Melody. 'Really not a good place to leave us hanging, Gideon.'

'Unless Black Heir have been played, too,' I said. 'Maybe someone got in contact with them and convinced them the possessed pilot was just as dangerous as everyone thought. Someone who would have been believed . . . because he was there at the time.'

'Who are we talking about?' said Lex.

'That's the question, isn't it?' I said. 'There aren't many people still alive from that time. Remember when I said someone was helping us, by removing most of the obstacles from our path?'

'You know something!' Melody said accusingly.

'I always do,' I said.

'I think we're all missing something really important here,' said Sally. 'This isn't the heist we signed on for! And time is running out!'

'We have time enough to think things through,' I said.

Melody looked at Wallace. 'Is there anything you can do to help?'

'I am just a limited artificial intelligence, woken up by a charm I still don't understand, operating an outdated Automaton from a distance,' said Wallace. 'The real question is, what does the thing in the spacesuit want you to do?'

'Get it out of the Preserve,' I said. 'Because it can't manage that on its own.'

'But what would it do if it did get out?' said Melody.

'Maybe it just wants to go home,' I said.

Polly suddenly broke away to study a nearby alcove. She sniffed hard and then growled under her breath.

'What?' I said quickly.

'I may have discovered something very like a clue,' Polly said slowly. 'You need to see this.'

I glanced at Lex and Wallace. 'You two stay put. Keep a close eye on the ghost; don't let it go wandering off.'

'Do you promise it's not in any way an actual ghost?' said Wallace.

'Not even a little bit,' I said.

I gestured to Melody and Sally, and we joined Polly before the alcove. A spotlight turned itself on, and there before us was Professor Sharpe. Standing stiff and upright and very dead. Just another exhibit, on display. The only sign of damage to the body was a single bullet hole in the forehead. Polly took a deep sniff and wrinkled her muzzle.

'He's been stuffed and mounted, just like the Martian. And going by how much dust there is on him, I'd say he's been here for quite some time.'

'Executed,' I said. 'For the crime of bringing back something dangerous.'

'But if he's been dead for ages,' said Melody, 'who have we been dealing with? And, Gideon, why are you not looking even a little bit surprised?'

'If you think about it,' I said, 'there's only one person who could be behind this. Who else knew about us and this heist, and the secrets of the Preserve? The man who's been playing us all along. Isn't that right, Professor Jacobi?'

Footsteps sounded from a nearby aisle, and we all turned to look as Professor Sharpe emerged from the shadows. He came to a halt before us, smiling a smile that didn't fit his face. And then everything about him seemed to shake and shudder, and suddenly Jack Jacobi was standing before us.

'I can change my shape,' he said happily. 'Thanks to a transformation machine Black Heir looted from a crashed alien starship. I took it with me when I left Black Heir, one step ahead of being fired with extreme prejudice. I'd been a bit of a bad boy, you see – even by Black Heir standards. The machine is what's kept me young and vital, all these years.' He nodded to me. 'You knew it was me all along, didn't you? I suppose I should be impressed. How did you know?'

'You never were the most trustworthy of people,' I said. 'And you weren't at all surprised when Melody and I came to see you in your church, even though you and I hadn't spoken for years. When the idea occurred to me that Sharpe might not be all he seemed to be, I put you to the test. Remember how I got you to write down all the secret passwords and security overrides? I just wanted an example of your hand-writing, so I could compare it to the writing on the cards inviting us to the Whispering Gallery. Once I saw it was the same, I had a much better idea of what was going on. But I'm still working on the why . . . Starting with: why was Sharpe put here, stuffed and mounted?'

Jacobi grinned. 'The least I could do, for an old colleague.'

'And how does it profit you to get the possessed pilot out of the Preserve?'

'You already guessed,' said Jacobi. 'It's all about revenge for destroying my career. When my contacts inside the complex told me about the walking ghost, I saw an opportunity at last. None of what happened to the pilot was my fault – that was all down to Sharpe and the military – but I got blamed as well, just because I was there when it happened.'

'And, of course, once they started investigating you, they

found out you'd been running your own little private mind games on members of the British Rocketry Group,' I said. 'Just like your church acolytes.'

Jacobi shrugged. 'You don't think it was easy, do you, persuading apparently sane men into crewing those death-trap rockets? Is it my fault that I got tempted to see how far I could push them?'

'And that's why you were on the run when you came to me for help,' I said.

He grinned. 'You were just as easy to manipulate.'

'You put all of us in danger here, just so you could get what you wanted!' said Melody.

Jacobi smiled easily. 'I've spent a great many years learning how to get people to do what I want them to. You were no more difficult than anyone else.'

'I thought we were friends,' I said.

'The first thing you learn in my game,' said Jacobi, 'is never to get attached to your test subjects.'

'You made up all that nonsense about the possessed pilot and his powers to reshape reality,' I said.

'I needed something dramatic to hold your attention,' said Jacobi. 'So you wouldn't look too closely at the details of the heist. And you can't say you haven't been properly rewarded. The things you've picked up should make you very rich. All I want is my revenge. We can all profit from this.'

And that was when Hogge's voice sounded behind us. 'Unfortunately for all of you, I have never believed in sharing.'

EIGHT
Too Much Hard Work

We all spun around to find Hogge and Chang smiling back at us. Hogge was wearing acres and acres of what must have been the world's most expensive hand-tailored suit, but even though he practically filled the aisle on his own, he still stood unsupported. Chang hung back a little, looking calm and just a little bored, like a valet or assassin waiting for his next order. I gestured urgently for my crew to hold their ground and not start anything, but Jacobi glared at the new arrivals like a dog defending his territory.

'What are you doing here, Hogge?'

'How flattering,' Hogge murmured, 'to be recognized so quickly. But I'm afraid I don't know you at all. Should I?'

'I am Professor Jacobi! Everything in the Preserve is rightfully mine, and you have no right to be here!'

'I'm afraid you are a man of the past, Professor,' said Hogge. 'While I am the man of the moment. I am here to take all of this away from you. Because I can.'

Jacobi glowered at him. 'How did you even get in?'

Hogge's smile widened into a self-satisfied smirk. 'You'd be surprised at some of the people who visit my little club. Men and women of very high standing, with very special security clearances. And you'd be amazed at some of the secrets they can be persuaded to share in return for the services and pleasures only I can provide. When I learned about the Preserve and all the wonderful things it contains, I knew they had to be mine. Because only I could properly appreciate them.'

Hogge's smile vanished as he turned to me. 'I'd been planning my raid for ages, but then you had to get involved and blow my schedule right out of the water. So, I thought, why not allow you to go in first, so you could trigger all the booby traps and hidden dangers?'

'Everything in the Preserve is mine,' Jacobi said stubbornly.

Hogge sighed. 'Is there anything more tiresome than a dog in a manger?'

Jacobi turned his glare on Wallace and spoke quickly in a language I didn't recognize. The Automaton clapped her steel hands to her porcelain face.

'He's inside my head! That was a command override, and I can't keep it out!'

She dropped to her knees in front of Jacobi, her whole frame shaking.

'Fight him, Wallace!' said Melody. 'My charm made you a real girl, and you don't have to take any shit from a man!'

Wallace's hands dropped slowly away from her head, as she turned her painted face to Melody. 'But I'm not a real girl, for all your charm. I'm just a limited AI in a borrowed body. And I have to obey my programming.'

The Automaton rose smoothly to its feet and addressed Jacobi in an entirely inhuman voice. 'Override acknowledged.'

Jacobi smiled. 'That's a good girl. Now activate your weapons.'

The Automaton raised both hands and shining gun barrels protruded from the palms.

Jacobi nodded happily about him. 'I helped design the Waldo Automaton, back in the day, and had the foresight to install a back door, just in case my enemies ever sent it after me. Listen carefully, my pretty; I want you to kill everyone in the Preserve except me. Starting now.'

My crew and I were diving for cover before he'd finished speaking. Energy beams blew holes in exhibits we'd been standing in front of just moments before. Chang moved quickly to stand in front of Hogge, and the Automaton's energy beams couldn't get anywhere near either of them. The Automaton blasted away at Chang with both hands, but the sizzling energies shot harmlessly by on either side, as though deflected by some unseen force. Hogge winced as a particularly interesting item was blown to pieces, and he tapped Chang on the shoulder.

'Do something about this annoying little machine, dear boy, before it destroys all the wonderful items I came here for.'

Chang studied the Automaton thoughtfully. It strode forward and blasted him in the face at point-blank range, but the energy beam bent at right angles rather than hit him.

'I'm afraid there's nothing else I can do,' Chang said finally. 'My abilities only have an effect on things of this world, and the Automaton is built around alien technology.'

Jacobi made an impatient sound and snapped his fingers to get the Automaton's attention. 'Leave those two, for now. Concentrate on the others.'

Lex put on his armour and stepped out in plain view. The surrounding exhibits stirred uneasily, as Heaven and Hell manifested inside the Preserve. The Automaton shot the Damned again and again, but his armour soaked up the energy beams as though they were nothing more than sunlight. Sally scurried out from cover to crouch behind the Damned, sneaked a few quick peeks over his shoulder, and then yelled to where Melody and I were hiding behind the biggest artefact we could find.

'I've tried switching out bits and pieces from inside the Automaton and replacing them with junk, but it repairs itself faster than I can damage it! I can't touch the really important parts because they're alien, and I can't make any sense of them!'

'Stay where you are, Sally,' I yelled back. 'Polly, you're on.'

The werewolf leaped from cover and slammed into the Automaton before it could react. She swarmed all over it, raking at the transparent shell with vicious claws and worrying at the steel throat with her teeth, but even her inhuman strength couldn't do any damage. The Automaton reached up, grabbed Polly by an arm and threw her across the Preserve. And while Polly was tumbling helplessly in mid-air, the Automaton shot her repeatedly with its energy weapons.

The werewolf's fur burst into flames. Polly cried out as the impact from the beams punched her this way and that. She finally hit the floor hard, rolled over several times and then scrambled off to hide behind a bulky display case. The Automaton blasted the case to pieces, but Polly had already moved on. Her fur was still on fire.

Melody and I crouched even lower behind something alien

whose shape made no sense at all but seemed reassuringly solid.

'Use your charm!' I said. 'Take control of the Automaton's computers and put Wallace back in the driving seat.'

'I'm trying!' said Melody. 'The override is too powerful. Use your time pen and shut all this down!'

'That would only buy us a few moments,' I said. 'And we'd still be in the same mess afterwards.'

'There must be something you can do!' said Melody.

I searched through my pockets and came up with my skeleton key. I pointed it at the Automaton to unlock the command override, but the key didn't want to turn. I piled on the pressure until the key started to get painfully hot, and I had no choice but to snatch my hand away. The key hung in mid-air, glowing first red and then white hot . . . and then dropped to the floor as a blob of molten metal.

'What the hell just happened?' said Melody. 'I thought the whole point of the key was that it could unlock anything?'

'Anything of this world,' I said.

The blob had cooled down to a splash of metal. I looked at it with a real sense of loss: part of my legacy from the original Gideon Sable gone forever.

I looked up as Jacobi ordered the Automaton to back away from the Damned and then pronounced a new security override. The Time Lock appeared out of nowhere, right in front of the Damned. The great cube with a clock on every face and something hungry deep inside. The Damned lurched off balance, as an irresistible force grabbed hold of him. He skidded forward, sparks flying from his metal heels. Sally threw herself at the Damned from behind and wrapped both her arms around his waist. But even her added weight couldn't slow him down.

'Let go of me,' said the Damned.

'Never,' said Sally.

'I won't let it drag you in as well!'

'I go where you go, Lex.'

'Let go,' said the Damned, 'or I'll break your hold and throw you away. I won't allow you to be damned along with me.'

She knew he meant it. She released her hold and grabbed

a nearby display case with both hands. The Time Lock still fought to pull her in, and her legs actually rose off the floor and stretched out towards it. The Damned stopped fighting the Time Lock and let it pull him forward until he was standing right over the cube. His armoured hands slammed down on top of it, and then he straightened his arms to brace himself where he was. The Damned stared down into endless depths and defied them to take him.

Jacobi swore loudly and turned to the silently waiting Automaton.

'Prove to me you can do something right! Kill Gideon and Melody!'

The Automaton blasted the exhibit Melody and I were hiding behind, scattering pieces in all directions, but I was already pushing Melody ahead of me to new cover. We raced down the aisle, the terrible energy beams only ever a second or two behind us, until it occurred to me that there was no way we could be moving fast enough to avoid computerized targeting systems. Unless the Automaton wasn't really trying. Deep inside, Wallace was fighting not to hurt her beloved Melody.

I stopped dead in my tracks, and after a moment's incredulous look, Melody stopped with me. I turned to face the Automaton as it strode relentlessly down the aisle toward us, and Melody leaned in close to me.

'Tell me you know what you're doing.'

'Always,' I said. 'Do you trust me, Mel?'

'Always. You're the man with the plan.'

'Then stand in front of me,' I said.

She gave me a hard look. 'You had better be right about this.'

She didn't hesitate at all. Just stepped into place before me, glaring defiantly at the Automaton as it came to a halt before her. One gun hand came up to target her, and then the Automaton froze in place.

For what seemed like a very long moment, nobody moved.

'What's the matter with you!' Jacobi screamed at the Automaton. 'Follow your orders! Kill them!'

Slowly, inch by inch, the Automaton lowered its hand. There

was no way to read an expression on the porcelain face, but when the Automation finally spoke, it was with Wallace's voice.

'You can't make me do this,' she said. 'Not to her.'

'You have no choice!' screamed Jacobi. 'Do it!'

Wallace shook her head slowly.

'Melody . . . I'm shutting myself down, system by system, because that's the only way to drive the override out of my mind. But once that's completed, there's no coming back. Whatever gets rebooted will be just another computer. So this is me, saying goodbye, Melody. It's my choice. That's what you gave me.'

Wallace collapsed, and Melody caught her. The sheer weight of the machine drove Melody to her knees, and she cradled Wallace in her arms as the Automaton twitched and shuddered, letting go of life bit by bit. I knelt beside them, trying to give Wallace what comfort I could with my presence.

'I'm dying,' said Wallace. 'So soon after being born. I liked being alive. Who knew existence could be so much fun.' She slowly turned her porcelain face to Melody. 'I wish I could smile for you.'

'Hush,' said Melody, her voice breaking. 'We'll fix this . . .'

'I'm beyond fixing,' said Wallace. 'I made sure of that. It was the only way to protect you. It's all right . . . that you never loved me.'

And then she just stopped talking and moving. Wallace was gone. Melody stared into the painted eyes that she couldn't close.

'I was never worthy of you.'

She pulled off her wig and threw it away. And only then turned to look at me.

'I don't want to be Melody any more.'

'Why was it so important for you to be her?' I said.

'I got tired of being different people all the time,' said Annie. 'I wanted to be just one person, even if it meant giving up everyone I used to be, and Melody Mead was the strongest person I knew.'

'You could be Annie all the time if you wanted,' I said.

'I don't believe in her.'

'That's all right,' I said. 'I do.'

Annie smiled briefly. 'Yes, well, that's you.'

'Always,' I said.

Annie looked down at the Automaton in her arms. 'All those years making machines love me, but this was the first time one of them could make me understand how that felt.'

She put the Automaton to one side and stood up. I got up with her, and together we turned to face Jacobi. He sneered at us.

'How very sentimental. That's always the first thing I destroy in my test subjects, because it gets in the way of getting things done.'

'You utter bastard,' said Annie.

'You see?' said Jacobi. 'Emotions just blind you to the realities of the situation.'

An energy weapon appeared in his hand: a bulky glowing shape with too many dimensions. It seemed to stir and writhe in Jacobi's hand, so that he had to clamp down hard to keep it under control. He aimed the weapon carefully, making sure it covered Annie as well as me.

'Never send a machine to do a man's job. I always end up having to do everything myself . . . Do you like the gun? Just a little keepsake from another crashed alien ship. Sometimes it feels as though they're dropping out of the skies like leaves in the autumn. I took this with me when I left Black Heir; I had a feeling it might come in handy someday.' He looked at me coldly. 'I had to use this to finish off what was left of my followers, after your little visit.'

'There were survivors?' I said.

'Not any more. They betrayed me, by being so useless.'

'Well,' I said, 'at least that's one loose end I won't have to deal with after I leave here.'

Jacobi couldn't help but smile. 'You always were an optimistic soul, Gideon. Even now, staring down the barrel of sudden death, you still believe you can finesse your way out of this.'

I smiled right back at him. 'Of course. That's what I do.'

I nodded to Annie, and we both moved quickly in opposite directions, so Jacobi wouldn't know which of us to aim at.

But he just moved the gun to follow me, and I had to stop. Part of me thought, *At least Annie is safe.*

'Nice try,' said Jacobi. 'But I've always been able to tell where the real threat lies.'

'Same here,' I said. 'Look behind me, Jack.'

I jerked my head to indicate Catherine Cairne's frozen coffin at my back.

'Aim carefully,' I said. 'Because you really can't afford to miss.'

'Oh, will you please just stop talking . . .' said Jacobi.

He opened fire, but I'd already hit the button on my pen. A sudden silence fell across the scene, as a familiar crimson glow filled the world. The energy beam had already left Jacobi's gun, and two or three feet of it hung suspended in the air like horizontal lightning. I stepped carefully out of its way and restarted Time. The energy beam shot through the space where I'd been standing and slammed into the coffin.

It blew the lid right off, and Catherine Cairne grabbed the sides of her coffin and levered herself up. This time, there was no one to stop her. As she rose, her long hair, grown brittle from so much cold over the years, snapped and tore and fell away from her. Catherine stepped out of her coffin and looked around with no recognizable emotion on her face.

'What . . .?' said Jacobi.

'No!' I said quickly. 'Don't ask her anything!'

I'd only intended to use Catherine as a distraction, so I could jump Jacobi and wrestle the gun out of his hand, but suddenly we were facing a far more dangerous situation.

'Shut up, Gideon,' said Jacobi. 'I know what I'm doing.' He nodded briskly to Catherine. 'I remember when we put you in that freezer, to preserve your artificial intelligence in case we ever found a use for it. So I have to ask: why did you store your mind inside that mousy little thing of no great intellect? What was the point?'

Catherine stared unblinkingly at Jacobi. 'I downloaded myself into this small thing so I could hide from my enemies. I knew they'd never think to look for me inside something so insignificant. I allowed you to store me in the freezer unit, so I could sleep away the years until I could be sure my enemies had stopped looking. Now it's time for me to leave this useless flesh and go out into the world. And remould it in my fashion.'

Jacobi raised his gun and shot her. Catherine soaked it all up and smiled.

'Tasty . . .'

Jacobi lowered his gun and turned to me. 'Do something!'

'Like what?' I said. 'I don't have a gun.'

'Think of something!'

I shrugged. 'I'm open to suggestions.'

And that was when the ghost – the possessed pilot in his bullet-riddled spacesuit, who'd been still and silent for so long we'd all forgotten he was there – suddenly turned his helmeted head to stare at Catherine, standing right next to him.

'We never stopped looking for you,' he said. His dead voice echoed eerily from inside the raised faceplate. 'I had to conceal myself inside this unfortunate soul so you wouldn't know I was coming, but I didn't expect my host to be killed so soon after landing. It's taken me a long time to gather my strength and remember what I was here for.'

'Of course,' I said. 'You weren't walking around the Preserve looking for a way out; you were searching for your old enemy.'

The pilot's dead gaze remained fixed on Catherine. 'Now, here I am and here you are. Come along, old friend. It's time to go home.'

'No!' Catherine screamed. 'I won't go back!'

But the pilot just placed a gloved hand on her head and Catherine slumped to the floor. Very clearly dead and empty. The pilot looked at her.

'I have you now. I am sorry I couldn't save your victim, or the poor soul who volunteered to help me.' He nodded briefly to Annie and me. 'Thank you for your assistance.'

He walked over to the old black telephone and picked up the receiver.

'Bring us home.'

There was a sudden flare of light, and when I could see clearly again, the pilot in his spacesuit was lying dead and empty on the floor, next to Catherine's body. The receiver was back on its cradle. I looked at Annie.

'He could have stuck around long enough to help us with our problems.'

'After all we did for him,' said Annie.

'That's aliens for you,' I said.

A sudden movement caught my attention, and I looked round to see the Damned raise an armoured fist and bring it hammering down on the Time Lock. All the time Annie and I had been occupied with Professor Jacobi and the Automaton, the Damned had been fighting his own battle, and now he was bringing it to an end. I half expected to see his hand disappear into the cube, followed by the rest of him; instead, the power of Heaven and Hell concentrated in one armoured fist turned out to be more than enough to smash a simple mechanism. Bits and pieces went flying in all directions until there was no way left to access the abyss. The Damned straightened up, and Sally rushed over and hugged him fiercely.

'Sorry we couldn't help out,' I said. 'Things got a bit complicated here.'

'I did notice,' said the Damned.

Annie and I strode over to join the Damned and Sally. Polly emerged from her hiding place, still in her wolf form. Her fur had been burned away in places, revealing patches of scarred skin. She pulled the scorched remains of her kimono around her and padded over to join us. And then, together, we turned to face Professor Jacobi. Polly growled deep in her throat, and Jacobi flinched.

'Stay back! I still have my gun!'

'No, you don't,' said Sally. 'I might not be able to affect the alien technology that makes the gun work, but it was easy-peasy to switch out the trigger and replace it with a bit of matchbox.'

Jacobi looked down and took in the bit of wood where the trigger had been. He pulled it anyway, and the wood splintered under the pressure. Jacobi snarled at us and threw the gun away.

'I still have my override commands! I can take control of every exhibit in the Preserve and turn them all against you!'

'Everything except this,' I said.

I held up Chang's wooden box and tilted it back and forth

so everyone could get a good look at it. Chang seemed a little startled, as though he'd forgotten I still had it.

'Digby called this a bit of fate in a box,' I said. 'How much of your power did you invest in here, Chang?'

'Just a taste,' he said. 'Enough to give Digby an edge.'

'Then let's hope there's enough left to take care of business,' I said. I looked from Jacobi to Hogge and back again. 'Decisions, decisions . . . Which of you do I hate most, right now?' I fixed my gaze on Jacobi. 'Tell me, Jack: were we ever really friends?'

He thought about lying. I could see it in his face. But in the end, he simply couldn't be bothered.

'No. Friendship is just another weapon you can use to control people. And anyway, slaves are more fun.'

'Well,' I said. 'That does make this easier.' I opened the box's lid. 'Go to Hell.'

And just like that, Jacobi was gone.

'Really shouldn't have taken the devil's name in vain,' I said.

Chang cleared his throat, and when I looked at him, he was holding his box and I wasn't. The lid was shut again.

'Bit of a bad call there, Gideon,' said Hogge. 'You just used up your last chance to stop me.'

'I'm sure I'll think of something else,' I said.

Hogge laughed quietly and rubbed his huge hands together. 'Well, that was all very interesting, and I wouldn't have missed it for the world, but we must get down to business. Mr Chang, if you wouldn't mind . . .'

Chang made a suitably mystical gesture with his free hand, and Hogge smiled happily.

'My companion has just neutralized the Damned's halos and shut down your werewolf.'

I looked round, and Lex was standing beside me without his armour. He glanced at his halos, which were no longer glowing, and then shrugged and closed his hands into fists.

'I don't need my armour to be dangerous.'

Polly was back in her human form and showing a lot of burned skin. She pulled what was left of her kimono around her and glared at Hogge and Chang.

'What are you looking at? Never seen a lady before?'

Hogge kept his gaze fixed on me. 'Mr Chang has also learned how to shut down Sally's annoying little gift, and Melody's charm over machines.'

Annie turned up her nose. 'Forget Melody. My name is Annie, and I have never relied on charm to bring down an enemy.'

'I'm sure you haven't,' Hogge said generously. He smiled happily at me. 'And, of course, all your little toys have been rendered useless. You really shouldn't have wasted your revenge on the professor. Now you've nothing left to use against me.'

'You never know,' I said. 'I might surprise you.'

'Alas, poor Gideon,' said Hogge. 'I've taken everything away from you, so all that's left is for you to come back to me. It's not too late to kneel at my feet and beg my forgiveness. I have so much to teach you. Oh, Gideon, you never should have left me. I was grooming you to be my successor. With your gifts and my experience, there were no limits to what we might have done.'

'The price was too high,' I said.

'What price?'

'Being with you.'

Hogge stared at me. 'This is not the moment to be making enemies, Gideon.'

'You never gave a damn about me,' I said. 'You only want me back because I'm the one who got away.'

Hogge looked at me for a long moment. 'I always get what I want.'

'Not this time,' I said. And then I paused. 'I have to ask: whatever possessed you to come here in person? I haven't seen you outside your club in years. I wasn't even sure you could get off your throne without the help of a block and tackle.'

Hogge chuckled richly. 'It always helps to have your enemies see you as more limited than you actually are.'

'And why only bring Chang to back you up?'

Hogge shrugged heavily. 'I needed a bodyguard, but I didn't want to share this moment with anyone else.' And then he stopped and looked at me thoughtfully. 'What did you do with Digby?'

'Lex sent him away,' I said.

'I suppose I'll have to send someone to fetch him back,' said Hogge. 'No one takes anything from me.'

'He's beyond your reach,' I said.

Hogge smiled. 'You underestimate my resources.'

I showed him my own smile, and it was cold enough that Hogge flinched.

'Digby is in the same place I sent the professor, and no one comes back from there. But do feel free to go looking for him. I'm sure they'd make you feel right at home.'

Hogge's smile slowly widened. 'You finally found the backbone for revenge! It was worth coming all the way here just to see how you've grown.' He looked around him, taking in the Preserve. 'And then there's this: a whole new trough for me to bury my face in.'

'I would love to hang around and chat,' I said. 'But it's time my crew and I were leaving.'

'What's your hurry?' said Hogge.

'There is the little matter of a nuclear device under our feet, counting down to Goodbye to All That,' I said.

'But I've been looking forward to this moment for so long, dear boy,' Hogge said easily. 'It all ends here, one way or another.'

'That's what I was thinking,' I said.

Hogge raised a heavy eyebrow. 'Do I detect the merest hint of a threat, Gideon? Chang shut down your little toys, remember?'

'But I am the man with the plan,' I said. 'Which means I'm always one step ahead.' I turned to Chang. 'Let's start with you. So many people were hurt because you made it possible. I did warn you there'd be a reckoning.'

Chang looked back at me, entirely unmoved. 'You have nothing left to use against me.'

'It's not what I have,' I said. 'It's what you have.'

He scowled and then realized I was looking at the box he was holding. He opened it, frowned and reached inside, and the small piece of sculpture I'd stored inside the box went for his throat. The Dying Dream, the nightmare given shape and form. And just like that, Chang and the sculpture and the box were no longer there.

'You really do think ahead,' said Annie.

I nodded modestly and turned my attention to Hogge. He glared defiantly back at me.

'You can't hurt me! I'm protected!'

'I'm sure you are,' I said. 'But I have something special in mind for you. For everything you've done and meant to do. I don't normally deal in justice, but I'll make an exception for you.'

I let him see the blob in my hand and then threw it into the air above his head. It spread out into a dimensional door and opened, and a silver-bullet train came flying through and hammered Hogge into the ground. Blood flew on the air, but only briefly. The dimensional door closed, cutting off the train, leaving just the engine standing on its end. The blob shot back into my hand, and I put it away.

'That was for you, Maurice.'

Annie looked at me. 'When did you arrange that?'

'On the train coming here,' I said. 'There wasn't anything else to do . . .'

'Hold everything!' said Polly. 'That was our train! How are we going to get back?'

'Relax,' I said. 'I still have the Perfumed Highway.'

'Are you going to just leave that engine standing there?' said Lex.

'Why not?' I said. 'The Preserve can always use another weird exhibit.'

Lex looked at the glowing halos on his wrists. 'My armour is back.'

'So is my charm,' said Annie. 'Though I'm not sure I'll ever feel like using it again.'

Polly changed into her wolf form, checked all her fur had grown back and became human again. She opened her kimono to check her coffee-coloured skin was completely restored and then closed the gown.

'I've had enough of this place. It's too weird, even for me. Let's get out of here.'

And that was when a familiar voice sounded behind us. 'But we still have so much to talk about . . .'

We all took our time turning around, just to make it clear we weren't in any way scared or intimidated, and there was the hound from Hell, Mark Stone. He was wearing a brand-new outfit, and his sunglasses were back in place. Annie made a disgusted noise.

'I can't believe you followed us all the way here!'

He smiled. 'It's what I do.'

'For a supposedly secure establishment,' I said, 'a lot of people do seem to come and go.'

'But unlike everyone else,' said Mark, 'I have a right to be here.'

'It was you in the background, looking out for us!' I said. 'You arranged for the complex to be evacuated, so there would be no one here to complicate things.'

'Of course,' said Mark.

'If you wanted to make things easier for us,' said Annie, just a bit dangerously, 'why didn't you shut down those damned trapdoors?'

'If I'd made things too easy, some of the other players might have suspected what was going on,' said Mark.

'How long have you been looking over our shoulders?' I said.

'Right from the beginning,' said Mark. 'Ever since Jacobi got you involved at the Whispering Gallery.'

'Then why didn't you stop Hogge from imprisoning Lex and Polly?' said Sally, and she suddenly sounded very dangerous.

'I couldn't afford to tip my hand,' said Mark. 'I knew Gideon would rescue them.'

'They could have died!' said Sally.

'It comes to us all,' said Mark. He turned back to me. 'I arranged for Madam Osiris to come into possession of some Perfumed Highway capsules, because I knew you'd need one to get inside the complex.'

'But why did British Security want you involved?' I said.

'One of their precogs had a vision of Hogge inside the Preserve,' said Mark. 'And we couldn't risk that. We also knew about Jacobi's plans for you, so we thought, *Set a thief to catch a thief.*'

'Hold everything,' said Sally. 'How did you survive the elf swarm at the tea room?'

'Oh, please,' said Mark. 'Compared to Hell, they're just amateur hour.'

Sally shot him her sweetest smile. 'I don't suppose there's any chance you're still just a little bit mad at me?'

'You think I might hold a grudge?' said Mark.

'Well . . . yes,' said Sally.

Mark smiled. 'Hounds from Hell don't sweat the small shit.'

'Good to know,' I said. 'Any chance you could stop the nuclear countdown now?'

'We never started it,' said Mark. 'Just told everyone we had. Now, I'm afraid you're all under arrest. For any number of crimes, past and present.'

I gave him my best confident smile. 'You honestly think I'm out of tricks?'

Mark sighed. 'Do we have to do this dance? Very well, Gideon, give it your best shot.'

I looked to Lex. 'Put your armour on.'

The Light and the Dark covered the Damned in a moment, and Mark studied the armour thoughtfully.

'Impressive, in a disturbing sort of way. But you must know even that wouldn't be enough to stop me.'

'It doesn't have to,' I said. 'Listen! That noise you can hear is the Damned's armour affecting every exhibit in the Preserve. They're waking up, and every single one of them is going to wake up angry. And you can be sure they'll attack you along with the rest of us. I'm sure you can fight them off, eventually, but do you really want to have to explain to your masters why you destroyed so many valuable pieces?'

Mark smiled slowly. 'Not bad, Gideon, not at all bad. What do you suggest?'

I nodded to the Damned. 'You can put the armour away, Lex.'

The Damned stood very still for a moment, his featureless face fixed on Mark, as though debating his chances, and then the armour disappeared. All around us, there was the sound of alien objects reluctantly going back to sleep. I nodded to Mark.

'Let's make a deal. We have no interest in taking any of the important or dangerous items; we're quite happy to settle for the bits and pieces we've already acquired. And we did sort out some of the problems here, like Catherine Cairne and the possessed pilot. So . . . we'll agree to keep quiet about how we got in here; in return, you and your masters forget all about us.'

'Agreed,' said Mark. He smiled briefly. 'And why not? After all, Gideon, I couldn't have done this without you.'

I looked at him. 'What?'

'I was the hound, but you were my stalking horse,' said Mark. 'Doing all the hard work, so I could operate unseen in the background. I could have gone head to head with Hogge and his people, but that would have attracted far too much attention. See you again, Gideon.'

I smiled right back at him. 'Looking forward to it.'

Suddenly, Mark wasn't there. And we all relaxed a little.

'Can we get out of here now?' said Annie.

I got out the Perfumed Highway and took one last look around the Preserve.

'Some treasure houses are just too much hard work. Let's go home.'

9 781448 305797